they won't demolish me!

by Roch Carrier
Translated by Sheila Fischman

ANANSI

Le deux-millième étage was first published in 1973 by Editions du Jour, 1651 rue Saint-Denis, Montreal

Published and translated with the assistance of the Canada Council and the Ontario Arts Council

Cover design: Roland Giguère

Typesetting by Annie Buller Typesetting
Printed by The Hunter Rose Company

ISBN: (Paper) 0-88784-328-X (Cloth) 0-88784-429-4
Library of Congress No: 74-75918

House of Anansi Press Limited
35 Britain Street
Toronto, Canada

1 2 3 4 5 6   79 78 76 75 74

the author and translator
dedicate this book to
Dennis Lee

There was a sudden thundering in Dorval's house. The soot and greenish moss trembled on the brick walls. When the tenants were sure the ceiling hadn't collapsed on their heads they raced to the stairs that went up to the next floor where the Marchessault family lived. Dorval had trouble carrying his great gelatinous belly; Cowboy, face pale and thin under his broad-brimmed hat, took the stairs four at a time, guitar in hand; Dupont-la-France wept and moaned.

"*Nom de Dieu de nom de Dieu!* this City is driving us mad. We need Nature, silence, fresh fruit!"

Mignonne Fleury was behind him, sharp heels hammering on the stairs; she had to hop because her skirt was very narrow, impeding her movement; downstairs, La Vieille complained without dropping a stitch.

"I'll be inside my coffin before I hear the last of their commotion!"

"You're right," said Killer Laterreur, one of the two Laterreur Brothers.

He and his brother Strangler were holding hands; they wouldn't leave their room. La Vieille dropped a stitch. Oh, she'd get out of this madhouse one of these days! She'd slam the door on the lot of them. She wasn't going to spend the rest of her life here. She'd seen mice again, two of them coming out of her armchair. And upstairs on the second floor

1

they were shouting and yelling. Her curiosity finally won out and the old lady remembered how to climb the stairs like a twenty-year-old.

All the anger in Dorval's house was directed at the Marchessault family; the old wooden staircase creaked and moaned under the heavy burden. Someone pushed the door open and a couple of babies' bottles fell to the floor and slammed into the wall.

The Nigger who lived on the ground floor came out of his room stark naked, smiled and went in again. No one knew why he smiled. They had heard nothing but silence as dark as his skin escape from his thick lips.

Cowboy was inspired, possessed. He picked up his guitar and the melody sprang from his lips and his hands all at once:

> With a noise like thunder
> The roof we live under
> Jumps into the sky -ay -ay -ay!
> Marchessault -oh -oh -oh
> You look like a cow -ow -ow -ow
> And your wife's a fat sow!

Hildegarde Marchessault was standing with her arms and head caught in the dress she was trying to pull over her massive body; as she waddled and wriggled her hips nothing was visible but her peach-coloured bloomers and huge thighs.

"What do you want?"

With many contortions the dress finally fell into place, concealing her bloomers and knees. She hastily fastened the buttons, hiding the two flaccid mountains that were visible inside the open neckline.

"Holy Virgin," grumbled Hildegarde Marchessault, "you don't send us anything but misery."

"Misery," Dorval echoed, "that always makes me bawl like a baby."

2

He wiped a tear from his cheek. Even if Hildegarde had buttoned the top of her dress he couldn't tear his eyes away from what he had seen.

"I'm too soft-hearted, but that doesn't give nobody the right to pull the roof off my house."

An angry choir agreed.

"Or push us around!"

"Or blow us up!"

Hildegarde sighed, profoundly bored. She gestured to the others to follow her.

Her big Barnabé was sitting at the long table in the middle of the kitchen, face streaked with grease and oil, eyes filled with tears. In the midst of stacks of unwashed plates, greasy cups and crusts and glasses was the motor of a car. Barnabé was caressing it as though it were a dog. The floor was piled with grease-stained sheets of paper. Dorval turned to face his tenants.

"You've all seen it! That wreck of a man is still playing mechanic games. Look at that hammer he's holding!"

"You think he should have a sickle too, I suppose," Hildegarde sneered.

"He's always frigging around with that motor and getting oil all over the place. This is a respectable house."

"Respectable," Hildegarde repeated, "sure it's respectable. If this is a respectable house what's a whore like Mignonne Fleury doing in it?"

With a deliberately provocative gesture Mignonne Fleury stroked the yellow ribbon that was perched in her red hair like a butterfly.

"At least I'm respectable enough to earn my own living without expecting nothing from nobody else."

The memory of Mignonne's embrace would soften any heart. Hildegarde noticed the men's eyes glowing with a luminous nostalgia:

"That one just opens her mouth and the men drop their pants!"

"Your Barnabé must've taken time off from his machine a few times to help you make those twenty kids of yours."

"Thirteen."

"Thirteen's enough," said Barnabé.

"Ah, shut your traps, you bunch of goddam capitalists! Hell, I'm too soft! In the war they always used to tell me, Dorval, you're too soft!"

He went over to Barnabé, who was slumping in his chair, and picked him up by the collar.

"You're going to get rid of that goddam motor or you and your gang are going to get the hell out of here and I'll replace you with a nice quiet couple that just makes a little bit of noise once a year when they try to remember what they used to do when they used to make love."

Hildegarde pulled Dorval's hands away from her husband's shirt.

"And where are we supposed to go? As soon as we set foot outside we aren't at home any more."

"Goddam capitalists! I kill myself trying to tell you the truth. You're being devoured by capitalism. It's a kind of cancer but you take care of it and feed it like a goldfish! You feed it off your own bodies."

"Dorval," said Hildegarde, "you don't have to insult us. Just because you know a little more than some of us you don't have to use it to insult your own people."

She wiped Barnabé's tears, spreading the black grime all over his face.

"They insult me and there ain't no better worker for ten streets around!"

"I never told you before," said Mignonne Fleury with a simper, "but me, I admire you."

"You're in my house now, not out on the street," Hildegarde warned her.

4

"Barnabé sweetheart, when I get a car are you going to fix it for me for nothing?" Mignonne replied.

"I'll bust it up for you free!" Hildegarde offered.

"Ah!" Mignonne sighed, "if only the poor man had some encouragement. He has the soul of an inventor, a mechanic."

When he heard himself being talked about so sweetly Barnabé revived and seemed to glow despite all his troubles.

"Today, scientific progress and technical advances have put us in the age of the computer." (He had forgotten that this was the first sentence in his correspondence course.) "Nowadays a man is a slave, not a man, unless he can dominate the machine." (This was the second sentence from his course.) "Dominating a machine means knowing how to take a motor apart and put it back together." (Third sentence.) "When I'm a mechanic I'll have work. I've been twiddling my thumbs here for nineteen months since my last job."

"Twenty-two," Hildegarde corrected him. "Count: I had Alphonsine and Nathalie, and there's another one in the works."

"I wanna be a mechanic."

He was dreaming. In the depths of his imagination he saw a house, a shining car, children with clean faces. Suddenly he raised his fist at Dorval and shouted.

"Yes, Dorval, I'm gonna be a capitalist. And you, you goddam communist, I'm gonna stick you in a jail where they won't even have bars, they'll have steel walls so your goddam revolutionary ideas'll be sealed in like jam in a jar."

Dorval looked at each of his tenants in turn and took pity on the human tragedy:

"You're beaten dogs." (Why was his voice so weak?) "You don't even bark to protect yourselves; when you bark it's just to ask to be kicked some more. You hope for happiness, but later. We need happiness right here and now, on our plates, in our beds."

5

Dorval left the Marchessault apartment, his belly prominent like one who was pregnant with truth. Hildegarde followed him, needing to hurt him:

"You preach and preach, like a priest turned inside out!"

"I'm too soft. Tenants like you ought to be thrown out with the garbage. I'm too soft."

"Barnabé, have you see the baby?"

Hildegarde had just remembered the baby's existence. She looked under the table, the chairs, outside, beneath the windows. Desperately.

"The baby?"

Her other children ran around the neighbourhood exploring back yards and digging through the garbage, but the baby? Who had just learned to walk? Her concern was aroused by a maternal foreboding: they could hear a soft object tumbling down the stairs with a dull sound that echoed at each step, bouncing up only to fall down again. The loud cry of a child burst into the silence where everyone was holding his breath. They all rushed out. Hildegarde imagined her baby with his arms broken, his neck snapped, his skull open: Barnabé was furious because his goddam kids always kept him from studying. He'd be out of work all his life and they'd have nothing but trouble: no house, no shiny car, and the brats would always have dirty faces. Dorval thought of the insurance premiums that he hadn't paid for a long time. Mignonne Fleury was glad she didn't have any kids. La Vieille forgot the ones she had given birth to. And Cowboy sang.

> He busted his little head, he did
> And his two little arms, yes his arms!
> And his nose, pouring blood, like a rose . . .

The baby wasn't hurt. Strangler Laterreur had picked him up. The child's mouth was pressed against the wrestler's chest and he was overjoyed, thinking he was back with his mother. Killer looked sentimentally at the child and placed his hand affectionately on his companion's shoulder. Hildegarde tore the child away, furious as a lioness.

At the bottom of the stairs Dupont-la-France waved his newspaper and announced in a voice that sounded as though he were sucking candies:

"They're going to demolish the neighbourhood!"

"What?" Dorval roared.

"What'll you do with your cockroaches if they tear it down?" asked Mignonne Fleury.

Dupont-la-France became enflamed.

"They ought to demolish the whole city, Montreal and all the rest. Bang! one bomb, that's all they need, a bomb to wipe out all the cities so we could see the earth again, good mother earth. Demolish the lot, *Mesdames et Messieurs*. Long live the return to nature! Long live the sun, fresh air, blue sky!"

"Now we get his ode to the apple!" Cowboy teased.

"Yes indeed. The apple contains water, the sky, fresh air, the sun—all clean and bright and pure. You can drink it all in apple juice. The apple was the heart of the Garden of Eden. Without the apple man is sad. He's an exile, a dying man who doesn't dare revive or die."

Mignonne Fleury interrupted the speech that they all knew only too well:

"Come on, Dupont-la-France, tell us the truth. When you see me on the stairs and push me against the wall, what do you ask me for when you whisper in my ear? A glass of apple-juice?"

"They're really going to demolish our neighbourhood."

Dorval winced as though he had a toothache.

* * *

The next day Dorval didn't leave his ground-floor window. He saw no bulldozer, no crane; he didn't sight a single stranger. The children sang and squabbled as they did every day. Dorval had never stopped to say, I like this street. Now he repeated it several times. Much later the lights went out in the windows one by one, and the last bursts of laughter could be heard from the children. Soon not one light would be on. No lights in the windows, only curtains soaked in night; from them would come coughs, children's crying, sighs and then a great silence. Night drowned all the bedrooms and secrets were sealed in sleep. Nothing remained of the engulfed city but a luminous backwash on the surface of the black sky. The brick palisade across from Dorval's window was diluted too. He waited, resisting the night. All alone, he drank several bottles of beer. He thought: We know what happens to a man if he falls to the bottom of the sea. But what happens to a man who falls into the depths of night?

Dorval stood in the window and pointed his finger at the houses on his street that he could not see, for the night was opaque and his own eyesight had been dimmed by alcohol.

"Instead of fighting you're all asleep, farting and snoring."

He brought his accusing fist to his chest which swelled beneath his crossed arms.

"Me, I'm alive," he proclaimed.

And his pride at being alive was vaster than the blackness of the night. He felt his drunkenness like a kind of joy. Dorval was drunk with happiness. The floor was breathing beneath his feet. The empty beer-bottles rolled and collided and there was the sound of breaking glass. He went to the stairs and with one step he was on the next floor. A giant able to leap over roofs, he tapped gently on the door of

Mignonne Fleury's room. A voice was silent. The bed-springs creaked nervously. The door stayed shut.

"Mignonne Fleury!"

The giant Dorval had yelled so loud that he could see the walls open, the ceiling fall onto his head, the beams crash onto his shoulders. Crushed beneath the débris, the giant Dorval laughed until his throat would burst, laughed as God will laugh at the end of time. He no longer saw the night.

Drunk, he slept peacefully at the bottom of the stairs down which he had rolled like a sack of oats.

* * *

A small man, squeezed into a grey suit worn out at the seat and elbows, pranced around Dorval who was snoring, quite confidently asleep. Without taking off his hat or letting go of the handle of his briefcase, the functionary continued to prance, wiping Dorval's forehead with a handkerchief he had wet at the cold-water tap. The big puffy face smiled in its contented sleep. The other man shouted invective at the sleeper, kicked him in the ribs. Dorval was fast asleep as the night. It was day now and the city's noises were increasing like the chirping of birds; Dorval remembered his childhood and his cackling hens.

"I promise you, you won't be defying our Municipal laws much longer. A week from now there won't be a piece the size of a handkerchief left of your house. One week from now this garbage-dump you call a street will be wiped clean and even your own smell will be gone. The whole thing will be disinfected. After you, everything will be new. That's progress."

As the functionary was reciting his lines, with all the conviction that habit had imposed on every syllable of every word, he was thinking, "This big half-asleep pig is a landlord and I'm still paying rent, even though I'm a hard-working, punctual civil servant. I'm condemned to pay rent every month." And he shouted,

"One more week and you'll disappear just like your dirt would disappear if you ever washed yourself!"

Cold water from the handkerchief ran into one of Dorval's ears and the damp shock opened his eyes. Was he in the hospital, sick, hurt? Someone was leaning over him. As he stood up he struck against the functionary's head and the man went flying as he tried to pick up his briefcase and hat.

"Sweet Jesus' baby bum! are you the doctor or the priest?"

"*Monsieur le Propriétaire,* I represent the Municipal Administration. Your house is going to be demolished."

"No!" Dorval roared. My house is staying where it is and me too, I'm going to stand on my own two feet. Like a man: on my own two feet!"

The functionary challenged Dorval scornfully.

"The whole area is going to be levelled. You've got one week."

"My house stays."

Accustomed to such reactions, as to an old refrain that he knew only too well, the functionary took his leave quietly:

"The Municipal Administration has already sent you nine registered letters about this . . ."

"Twelve . . ."

". . . in the last two years."

". . . thirty-seven in the last two years and a half. Do you know what I do with those letters from the Municipal Administration? I throw them in the fire. They aren't even good for wiping my behind. The stink poisons my crabs."

He kicked and the functionary sailed into the air, his hat flying and his briefcase releasing all his papers which took off like freed birds.

10

"Down with destroyers of the little guy!"

The functionary picked up his hat but he left his papers behind, and ran to the door where another charge exploded beneath him. This time he didn't have the courage to re-capture his hat. Behind him, breathless and choking with the effort, Dorval was threatening to rape the entire Municipal Administration.

"To hell with the capitalists!"

Dorval's face was contorted as though an egg were stuck in his throat.

"We've resisted the rats and we're going to resist the capitalists too!"

The functionary was proud of the bicycle-ride he took every Sunday after Mass. The exercise had kept his legs young. Otherwise he would have had to put up with a great many sore backsides.

Dorval stopped. His own legs could no longer support him. His stomach had the weight of a barrel of beer and his head seemed to have been dropped in it like an aching stone. In one final effort he found the strength to whisper to the grocer behind his fruit-stand.

"It's the beginning of the Revolution!"

"The Revolution? Don't look like a very good start to me."

"You're shaking, old man, because you sell the rotten apples and eat all the good ones. After the Revolution . . ."

"After the Revolution my goddam apples will still rot!"

A huge laugh lifted Dorval's sagging chest and propelled him in a strong, jerky run to his house. All the beer he had drunk the night before turned to laughter and his bursting voice, his foam-topped waves of laughter, filled the entire street.

Mignonne Fleury was going out. She walked faster to avoid Dorval. A tall, thin, red-haired man was with her. He turned his head.

11

Dorval went into his house, furious, and angrily slammed the door. He shouted (to God? to mankind? to Mignonne?):

"No! You won't demolish me!"

* * *

That evening the Maurice Richard Arena was swollen with anger. The crowd shouted its raging indignation. The Laterreur Brothers, flung to the floor in the center of the ring, were being turned into martyrs by two Russian wrestlers, Titov and Papov, ex-butchers who had been sentenced to Siberia for excessive violence. They had escaped on foot.

"No! No!" the crowd pleaded.

The spectators asked God not to allow two atheistic communists to defeat two Catholic French Canadians.

In his corner, Titov climbed onto the top rope and, hurling himself forward, he jumped and landed with both feet on Strangler Laterreur's chest. When the Russian's feet touched the French Canadian's chest, twelve thousand spectators gasped. But the bones of the wrestler's rib-cage hadn't been crushed. The crowd breathed again, got to its feet and with one unanimous cry thousands of fists were raised against Titov and Papov, against barbaric Russians, against Moscow and its allies. Mocking the threats and insults Papov took hold of Strangler, dragged the big heap of soft flesh to the ropes and twined the flabby arms around them. Strangler Laterreur was crucified.

"No!" the crowd implored when Titov, with an angry gesture, began to grope with his fingertips in his long mass of hair, seeking the blinding grease with which he usually ended his fights: the grease burned his adversaries' eyes. Wrestlers who had been given this treatment howled with pain, tried to

12

rub their eyes out of their sockets; laughing, Titov and Papov dodged the blows of the blinded men who finally, in despair, hurled themselves out of the ring. Titov and Papov were the fiercest wrestlers in history.

The crowd began to climb down through the seats to the ring. Insults! Curses! Howls! they weren't going to allow godless communists to cause so much pain to free French Canadians.

With complete contempt for the crowd, Titov and Papov coated the eyes of the Laterreur Brothers with grease; as it burned them they twisted and turned as though surrounded by flames. Not just their eyes but the entire bodies of the Laterreur Brothers had been consumed by the fire of the deadly grease. The Russians' toothless gums were opened in a criminal smile. Powerless and suffering, the Laterreur Brothers ran into the ropes and bounced back as though impelled by a powerful catapult. They collided face to face and fell to the mat unconscious.

Now the crowd was surrounding the ring. Fists raised, the men invited the Russians to come down and fight. The women were thinking: "It's like labour pains." Cartons of french-fries, shoes, umbrellas, hats, Coke bottles, matches, newspapers, pills, Tampax, money, a set of false teeth, a raincoat and a cane were flung into the ring. Beneath the avalanche Titov and Papov were smiling.

Killer Laterreur, nearly dead, whispered to Strangler who was breathing his last:

"What's the time?"

The dying man turned to look at the clock that hung above the ring and said:

"We're going to be late."

The two dying men got to their feet abruptly, hurled themselves at Titov and Papov, tied up arms and legs like a gigantic knot in a ball of string and the Russians dropped to the mat like two enormous poached eggs. The crowd leaped to its feet again, demanding harsher punishment for the Russians. But like true French-Canadian gentlemen the Laterreur Brothers did not take advantage of the Russians' weakened position.

"Kill 'em! Eat 'em raw!" roared the crowd.

The Laterreurs jumped out of the ring and disappeared. The crowd had just carried off a victory they had never dreamed of and they celebrated it with loud shouts and hearty embraces.

Still in their trunks, the Laterreurs ran to their old Packard which whined in pain as they got in.

"You think we done all right, I mean knocking down Titov and Papov like that?"

"Sure."

"It wasn't in the contract."

"No, I guess you'd'a rather got beat to a pulp, eh brother? Me, I'm fed up with getting beat up on contract."

"And I don't like it when you get yourself hurt."

Tenderly, Strangler wiped the sweat from Killer's brow.

When the Laterreur Brothers, wearing their trunks and dripping with sweat, came into the kitchen filled with tobacco-smoke, Dorval said to all the tenants who were waiting there:

"You got to choose: either be men or a bunch of crap that gets thrown out with the garbage."

Mignonne Fleury stood up:

"Even if I wanted to I couldn't be a man."

"Me neither," said La Vieille.

"And how about me," Madame Marchessault protested, "do you think I could?"

"We," said one of the Laterreur Brothers who, hand in hand, filled the doorway with their hairy sweating mass, "We want to be men."

Dorval had to keep bringing the discussion back to his subject; it kept leaping around like a crazy calf.

"We have to choose: Resistance or demolition."

"As far as I'm concerned," said Dupont-la-France, "I wish to protest. First, because I'm French. Then, I simply don't agree that an entire population should be kicked out in the street just because their houses are old. Of course there are advantages to having things new. But they'll get old, whereas what is already old will not."

"Now about you, Barnabé Marchessault, are you going to join the Resistance?"

Barnabé looked at Hildegarde, looked down at the floor, scratched the back of his neck, coughed, looked at Hildegarde, threw out his little chest and his breath of a voice joined the tobacco-smoke.

"Well, uh, if they demolish it's so they can build and uh, if I study it's so I can learn and uh, if they build it'll make jobs. If I got a trade, my mechanic's papers, I'd uh, have a job!"

"Vive la démolition!" Hildegarde proclaimed.

Dorval, pale and trembling, jumped onto a chair.

"You goddam Marchessaults, you can bugger out of here right now, this minute. Out on the street, and take you twelve goddam brats with you! Out!"

He wiped the sweat from his mustache and in the silence his face regained its normal colour.

"How about you, Nigger?" he shouted.

Without leaving his room the Nigger replied with a smile that suggested the happiest man on earth.

Dorval went over to Marchessault:

"No, I won't kick you out in the street. That's how the capitalists carry on, kicking people out in the street like they'd throw out an old kleenex."

He stared at his tenants one at a time:

15

"Are we going to form a Resistance?"

Each one acquiesced in silence, making a gesture with his head.

"Vive la Résistance!"

He opened the door of his refrigerator which was filled with bottles of beer.

"Help yourselves! But be polite. La Vieille first."

* * *

A few days later a political ceremony brought together at the corner of the street a Delegate of the Delegate of the Mayor, a Delegate from the construction workers' union, a Representative of the Delegate of the manual labourers, a Delegate from the non-union construction workers, a Delegate from the police, three Delegates from the banks, a Delegate from the American consulate and Delegates from all the political parties. After the speeches they were going to have a discussion at Queen Elizabeth's Hotel.

When they saw these strangers the people who lived in the neighbourhood stopped, bags of groceries or babies in their arms. They listened. By chance, Dorval was passing by the group. He listened too, then cried out,

"No, you'll never demolish me!"

The Delegates looked up and grimaced in disgust; the people from the neighbourhood smiled with a certain embarrassment because Dorval had just shouted aloud in the open air of Montreal a secret wish of which they were all a little ashamed. The neighbourhood people would have liked to go on living in the houses that were now part of the fabric of their lives, where they felt less ill-at-ease than anywhere else and where they were free because they could open and close their doors to whomever they chose. They weren't strangers in their own house, but they would probably be exiled now to far-away parts of the city where the houses seemed to belong to no one. Dorval was getting worked up and the Delegates were using their little lace handkerchiefs to wipe away the insults he hurled at them.

"Bunch of goddam capitalistic pirates! Why do you want to give us these new houses? Charity? If there was some charity in your lives you wouldn't be so rich now. You can demolish my house whenever you feel like it because you're the Administration. And you'll build me another house just as you like because you're Big Business. You'll sell it to me at the price you decide on because you're Commerce. And me, I'll borrow the money at your price too because you're the Bank. You haven't got any more respect for us than you got for a piece of toilet paper. When I look at you it's easy to see you haven't got a heart: you're all stuffed full of guts from scalp to toenails. But us, here, in this neighbourhood of ours, we got hearts. That's why you can't demolish us. Me, I got a heart too. My head's stuck on top of my heart, I got my legs down under it and they can take me far away where I won't smell your capitalistic stink. And out in front, right there where it belongs, I got a prick that points in the right direction. We got nice big bellies just like you, you goddam capitalists, but it's because us, we've got big hearts."

Dorval went along the Petite-rue-du-bon-curé-Poisson as he uttered his soliloquy, with all the gestures of a Roman orator in the forum. As a matter of fact he had left behind the political ceremony when the Delegate of the Delegate of the Mayor looked up from the speech that somebody had written for him, trying to make his voice louder than Dorval's.

"On official occasions when the Administration is officially announcing that it is undertaking an indispensably modern and progressive project, there is always opposition. Officially, the Administration believes that opposition is

17

good for democracy. If there is no opposition a party can't claim to be in power. Long live the Administration, long live the opposition and long live democracy!"

That evening Dorval, watching his television screen, saw the Delegate of the Delegate of the Mayor:

"On this official inauguration day I have the honour as the Delegate, the official Delegate, of the Delegate of the Mayor, to come here to inaugurate the inauguration of this construction project."

In the rocking chair he had bought because it was something like the one his grandmother had rocked in during the last years of her smiling old age, Dorval intoned the syllables, *"Ré-sis-tance, Ré-sis-tance."* Gradually the chair began to move more slowly, the syllables stayed longer on his tongue and he fell asleep. Outside, the neighbourhood was already demolished by the thick and heavy night.

When the first ray of light struck his face he awoke in surprise as though he had suddenly touched the bottom of an unreal gulf. He jumped to his feet, wiped the last grains of sleep from his eyes, sad already because during the night he had not been given any sign of hope.

"Baptême! If a man doesn't even get to dream when he's asleep he can't do a hell of a lot when he's awake."

Touching with his big fingers the disorder of his hair, his thoughts and the time, he went to stand on the doorstep of his house to assure himself that the street hadn't been destroyed while he slept. Standing there he was completely liberated from the night when he saw the houses still standing close together, supporting one another. They looked so pretty in the light of the new day! They looked as though they wanted to live for a very long time.

The street smelled of morning. Dorval filled his lungs with the smell, which was very strong here in this air that was the very source of his life. The street had the smell of the people who lived there, before they woke up, before the shouts of impatient mothers and the cries of children. He placed his hands on his torso and they moved in a delectable caress. In reality it was less his body that he touched than the brick of the houses on his street, the gray pavement that had been refreshed by the morning dew, the silent sidewalk: all that was part of his body.

As for the distant City, Dorval knew it like a newspaper that he would leaf through with boredom. The morning became very bright.

* * *

Trucks came and stopped in front of each door. When they went off towards the unknown City people were afraid; no one dared to set off empty-handed. No one abandoned his past: they carried all they could in order to re-create it elsewhere. They tried to lock it up inside their suitcases and trunks.

The trucks were filled with piles of scratched furniture, chairs with broken feet, armchairs with the stuffing coming out of the torn upholstery that smelled of children's urine, lamp-shades with holes in them, rusted tricycles, maps, saucepans, old suitcases that had never travelled, cardboard boxes, framed pictures of sad-faced saints or exotic landscapes, baby-carriages with invisible sniffling babies in them, bundles of newspaper tied up with string, and mattresses, mattresses, and bed-springs that looked like barbed-wire fences, mattresses yellowed by urine and sweat, hollowed by love, piled-up chairs, beds, tires, stoves where years of cooking fat melted in the sun, refrigerators, cardboard boxes with shreds of clothing hanging out. The trucks filled up. It seemed to Dorval that the demolition of the neighbourhood had already begun. The children were upset, dishes were clattering, drawers fell out of chests. The truck-drivers, climbing out of doors and windows, collided with weeping children and with other children who danced with delight as they climbed up the stacks of objects piled into the trucks; babies howled, forgotten in laundry baskets, and the women were disgusted at the truck-drivers' coarseness. Cigars in their mouths, the husbands waited. When the trucks were full the children found places for themselves among the piles of luggage along with the old people, while the women sat in the cabs with the drivers who raged at the crying babies; the husbands climbed onto the running-boards and ashes from their cigars fell onto their faces. The trucks growled, started slowly and painfully, with great effort, as though they had to pull out roots that were planted deeply in the neighbourhood; then the wheels turned more freely and the trucks, bent under their burdens, set off in a cloud of arms waving good-bye, with shouted good wishes that nobody believed in.

An old man was walking along on the arm of his tiny old wife. Both were wearing their best clothes and they seemed to be taking their Sunday stroll. Dorval had watched them for years, walking and making comments to each other in a low voice. He watched them as they came closer.

"Me," he said, "they aren't going to demolish!"

"We're always demolished in the end," the old man replied.

"My husband is always right," his wife agreed.

Dorval imagined that he would see them return as they had on Sundays in the past, their baggage following them in a silent procession: old chairs, old coats, old umbrellas, their old bed.

He turned towards his house which he would never leave: La Vieille, Dupont-la-France, the Laterreur Brothers, Mignonne Fleury, Cowboy and upstairs, Hildegarde and Barnabé Marchessault and their thirteen children were all standing at their windows watching the great displacement. When he looked at his house filled with all his tenants it seemed very beautiful, more beautiful than a fine apple-tree laden with fruit.

Still inhabited by all his tenants, who had not yet abandoned it, his house resembled a ship with its crew, preparing to cross a stormy sea.

"Goddam bunch of capitalists!" he shouted at them. "Listen to me. I'm reducing your rent by a buck a week!"

The cry had sprung from deep in his soul.

"And today I'm offering you free beer. But don't get carried away, you goddam capitalists! You exploit me. Always exploiting me . . . but today's a holiday."

There were cheers for Dorval from every floor in the house. Dancing and applause. Dupont-la-France declined the invitation.

"Beer, always beer. It's a chemical, full of poison. Why are we never offered something healthy to drink?"

"Apple-juice," replied the others with one voice, even the children.

"Chemical poisoning," said Dupont, "is part of a vast political conspiracy. First poison the people through chemistry, then reduce them to slavery."

"Me," said La Vieille, "I'll turn down a beer when they put me in my coffin, not before. To hell with my knitting!"

Marchessault came down the stairs dragging his feet:

"Me, I want to forget that goddam motor."

"Children," Madame Marchessault ordered, "out from under my skirts. There's nothing for you down there. When I was your age I had other ways to warm myself up. Go on, get lost! Go outside and run. We're celebrating!"

"They won't demolish us," said Dorval.

* * *

21

That evening the Marchessault children came tumbling down the stairs, drinking the dregs from beer-bottles; the babies called for their mother who didn't hear them. Barnabé Marchessault cried louder than his children, as he called for Hildegarde. He thought she had run away in a moving van. She had never liked this house. She had spent her childhood in a basement with her eyes, as she put it, on the sidewalk, and living on the second floor made her dizzy. Barnabé tried to summon his wife by hammering on his motor, howling, tearing the pages out of his correspondence course and throwing them out the window.

Dorval had drunk a lot and it felt as though it was his head that was being hammered. He decided to go up and see Barnabé.

The Laterreur Brothers were asleep in their room, affectionately entwined and snoring like enormous pigs. Dorval closed the door on their amorous slumber. The night weighed on his shoulders like a barrel of beer. He hoisted himself up the stairs. Ah! Ah! Hildegarde Marchessault was whinnying in Dupont-la-France's room. Dorval bent down to look in the keyhole. For once Dupont was quiet, dying with pleasure between Hildegarde's legs. Mignonne Fleury's door opened behind Dorval. Dorval stood up again. Dupont came out of Mignonne's room, carrying his shirt and doing up his pants. So it wasn't Dupont who was making Hildegarde moan. Mignonne closed the door on Dupont.

"You aren't the only one in Montreal; I gotta earn my living too."

Who was the man beneath whom Hildegarde Marchessault was enjoying herself so much? Dupont opened the door to his room, went in and after several cries had been uttered, Dorval saw an unknown man come out.

"Hey you; I never seen you before," said Dorval, "but the beer's free today."

"Thanks. Thanks a hell of a lot but me, I don't drink. Never touch a drop. But women! *Hostie!* That's what I go for. Somebody give me Mignonne Fleury's address. *Vierge!* Maybe you didn't know me before but you're sure as hell gonna get to know me now. I'll be back!"

"That wasn't Mignonne Fleury, it was Hildegarde Marchessault."

"What the hell, I'll be back! *Hostie!*"

The unknown man took off, singing loud enough to drown out a celestial choir:

> There was a poor man
> In his poor little house
> And he screwed his poor wife
> Pretty poorly.
> With his poor little tool
> On his poor creaky bed
> And he made her a kid
> That lived a poor life.
> It's a hell of a life
> No pleasure, no fun.

Dorval pleaded with Mignonne through her closed door.

"It's a holiday today. Why won't you let me in?"

"Go knock on the devil's door. He's the only one that'll let you in."

Next door in La Vieille's room Cowboy was searching for a tune on the strings of his guitar. Dorval put his ear against the door:

> Tomorrow I'll be on the road
> That takes me back to you
> Tomorrow we'll be holding hands
> Beneath a sky of blue.

Dorval pushed the door cautiously, as though he were afraid of breaking the song:

> You'll take flight in my hands
> High, high over the sky . . .

La Vieille was sitting on the floor, like a child surrounded by her dolls. The floor was dotted with empty bottles. She was ripping out her knitting as though unravelling time itself. The wool was tangled. With a look as vast as life she contemplated the stitches that were being undone. Dorval closed the door gently. Then he started to climb the last stairs.

Why was he touring his property like this? Why did he need to see his tenants, look at them as a gardener looks at his flowers? He loved them. The stairs were interminable. Dorval had grown too fat. He loved his house too. It was the hole he had punched in the universe and it belonged to him.

Among the children sleeping on the floor and the others who were sucking at beer-bottles, he saw Marchessault slumped over his motor and sobbing into the oil. Dorval said nothing and went downstairs again. He listened, breathless, as he stood on the stairs; life made gurgling sounds like an enormous digestive process.

At the end of the corridor on the ground floor the Nigger's door was open. Dorval approached. The Nigger was naked. His skin glistened in the shadows.

* * *

From farther and farther away electric stars were winking at the street lights. Dorval struck against the silence that was as hard as a wall. The pavement had contracted. The houses seemed shrunken, as though they were resisting some powerful wind. Dorval felt as though he were far away. He

24

had already experienced the clawing at the soul that people feel in a foreign country. His nostalgia was the nostalgia of those who had gone away in the trucks with their children, their furniture and their lives. The thought of them fell on Dorval like a heavy snowfall that was invisible but sad.

"They won't demolish me!"

Dorval started. His own voice seemed to have come from behind him.

A door was gaping open. Children had lived in this house, and a big pale guy without a job, and a woman who looked like a bearded whale. Her big pale husband looked like a bone that had been removed from her. The same family lived on all three floors in the house: they were all called Brûlotte: Elzée, Marc-Aurèle, Becycle, Antonifle, Marius, Théorigène. They were all brothers or cousins. A few wives too, all of them whales. Dorval turned on the light. There were big stains on the walls where the cupboards used to stand, because you don't paint behind them. The floor was littered with garbage: banana-peels, crusts of bread, cigarette butts, old underpants, broken bottles, rags, jam-jars, an old sofa with its insides cut out. Dorval turned on another light and climbed up the stairs. This empty house, its silence, gave him the sensation of being somewhere very high. It was a sort of dizziness. Dorval moved carefully, very carefully, up the stairs, as one would cross a river on a tree-trunk that might be rotten. With his foot he pushed aside pages from old newspapers, broken plates, crushed something—a pair of glasses; a dress was hanging on one of the doors. The floor was soft and every time he took a step the walls seemed to move.

"It's all going to collapse; when there were people here it was just habit that held up this stinking mess."

The old wood and plaster and brick had imbibed an odour of rot that had surged up from deep in the earth. There were probably insects and rodents turning mouldy

along all the girders. There was the warmth of brick and
macadam and tar. He was outside, on a balcony that he ex-
plored with the tips of his toes. In this night everything was
on the point of collapse. He moved forward, using his hand
to guide himself along the sticky wall. A door. He pushed it.
Small animals with claws scampered away. His hand moved
along a wall covered with torn wallpaper and found another
door-knob. Another black room. His cautious foot struck
against a step that led him through the night that was like a
polluted spring. Where did the night end, the staircase begin?
His outstretched hand touched only a damp void. The floor
lurched like the deck of a ship. Dorval stopped.

"Man isn't an animal that's meant for solitude."

In the center of the night Dorval was in the black belly
of Montreal; he thought that men build their cities so they
won't be alone: they surround themselves with walls so they
can't see the great endless night or the great endless day that
is even more dizzying; men surround themselves with walls as
trees surround themselves with other trees, each one scatter-
ing its seeds with the generosity of despair. And men make
walls of children and children make walls of fathers and
mothers and old people.

"They won't demolish me."

Suddenly there was a yellow light. Leaning against the
wall were two long-haired, dirty adolescents who looked at
him accusingly. Her blouse was unbuttoned. The boy moved
closer to her and to provoke Dorval he caressed her breast
with his fingertips.

"Ah!" Dorval thought, "their eyes are so pretty before
they turn into weeping cows."

Then, aloud:

"I'm looking for the exit."

"We're looking for a meaning for our life."

"When you've lived long enough you put your feet on

26

your neck and get out as fast as you can without asking directions."

"The flowers will take power," said the girl.

"The exit?"

"We're getting what we can out of life before it makes us too sad," said the boy.

"And too ugly," the young girl added.

"The exit?" Dorval insisted.

"There's no way out . . ."

The boy's hand closed over the girl's breast; it seemed to Dorval to shine brighter than any light.

His big rounded back swung silently through the night. He wandered again through stairways where the night climbed up and down; he struck against walls; as he continued through the gaps in the night he suddenly entered the deserted street, the dead street that would take him back to his house. It too could lead him elsewhere.

* * *

On the morning of that too silent day the huge beak of a mechanical crane was suspended over one of the neighbouring houses. It had arrived in the night and Dorval hadn't heard a sound. He shot out of his house to give the crane the first kick of the day but he noticed another one at the end of his street, its back threatening a house that almost touched his own. Everywhere there were mechanical cranes waiting to bite. The neighbourhood houses would collapse in a cloud of dust and crushed bricks, with the cries of beams that would shatter like bones; the neighbourhood would look like a gigantic pool of dried vomit where chewed-up bits of yesterday's life would still be recognizable. Dorval looked at the garbage, his stomach burning as though he himself had thrown out all this decay.

27

"They won't demolish me!"

He stepped very cautiously, as though the débris had already been spread out over the street. Most of the people had closed their doors, very carefully. It was what they did when they were going away for some time. Cranes had invaded the neighbourhood. Why had God made the light so beautiful on such a day? Dorval closed his eyes. A motor rumbled.

"This is death."

The silence extended everywhere through the neighbourhood; it quivered and tore. The walls trembled. Everywhere motors were roaring.

"This is war!"

He went home. A bulldozer was waiting in front of his door. The Nigger, dressed as though he were on his way to his own funeral, was standing to one side. He was standing as straight as a sergeant, and smiling.

"Did you see it come?"

The Nigger continued to smile.

"You didn't do anything to stop it? Goddam Nigger!"

The Nigger smiled and went back to his room. Dorval walked around the bulldozer, the mass of steel without a brain that would charge and pillage on command and never know why. He leaned against the blade. The mass of dead steel was pushing him, even though the bulldozer was frozen in its immobility.

"Goddam machine, heartless just like the capitalists. You're all set to run over my back but me, I'm going to resist. I've got a tough body, you'll see. You'll see my brains are in the right place. I'm no more scared of you than I'm scared of the good Lord or the Devil."

"If you keep going like that the bulldozer's going to cheer." Madame Marchessault was choking with laughter. Barnabé's head appeared beside her.

28

"Instead of trying to scare it we ought to take it away from under our feet."

"How?"

"By using our brains."

His thirteen children jumped on the back of the iron horse and began to tease it and worry it, trying to make it groan. They would have liked to make the big beast move right across the City. Marchessault, filled with knowledge from his correspondence course, lifted himself into the cab, pushing the children away. He pulled handles, pushed levers. The bulldozer was silent. Marchessault slapped a crying child. He turned keys, pushed handles, shook pedals. The thing stayed dead, like ice. He jumped to the ground, to the front of the machine, and stuck a crank into its big belly. The crank awoke some gurgling sounds but the strength of the machine remained asleep. Marchessault turned the crank, turned and turned, desperately. He struggled as though he were trying to raise the entire earth with block and tackle.

"What kind of courses are you taking, mechanics or knitting?" Dorval asked.

Marchessault's arms had turned soft but he kept turning the crank; his spine was melting like butter. Sweat pouring down his face, he fell to his knees before the machine.

"Impotent!" Hildegarde shouted.

He no longer had the strength to answer her insult. He could only remember. The night before, Hildegarde had babbled like an astonished child as she lay under him.

"Good for nothing!" Hildegarde shouted.

Marchessault burst into tears.

"It's that farmyard full of kids that howl all the time when I'm trying to study. It's all their fault."

The more he rebelled the stronger he became.

"It's big fat Hildegarde's fault." He distributed kicks and clouts among his children.

29

"When Hildegarde's around I can't see nothing but her big tits and then I can't study."

"Marchessault," Hildegarde protested, "you don't have to confess your whole life. Dorval isn't the *Curé.*"

Barnabé pulled out the crank. Hildegarde was leaning out the window. Her breasts were hanging in the neckline of her dress in a shadow that Dorval thought was lighter than light. Hildegarde let him look.

"If the kid hadn't made a boat out of the pages of my correspondence course I could've started that bulldozer."

Dorval grabbed Barnabé by the hair:

"Do you think the world's going to be better off if you figure out how to start up that motor?"

In the window Hildegarde was laughing like an enormous crow:

"Oh boy! Look at Marchessault and Dorval! They think they can improve the world and they can't even get a fart out of a motor!"

"If you're talking about Heaven on earth," said La Vieille, "I'll be seeing it when they nail me inside my coffin, not before."

"If you want to last till spring, La Vieille, you'd better save your breath," Hildegarde advised her.

"Life on this earth could turn out to be all right," Dorval mused.

The Nigger smiled in his doorway.

"Laterreur!" Dorval shouted.

Chests bare, arms around one another, the two athletes appeared at the window.

"We need you to . . ."

Dorval was about to ask them to help move the bulldozer.

"Get lost," he said; "go back and play with your dolls."

"Dorval," Killer said, "you shouldn't insult two champions."

"You're never a prophet in your own country," Strangler added.

"I'll take care of it myself," Dorval announced.

He leaned against the wall, facing the bulldozer, having made up his mind to stay there as long as the machine. The great beast pretended to sleep. But behind its iron eyelids it was dreaming. The cold immobility was deceptive: the bulldozer was preparing its attack.

"If you want to put some life into that bulldozer why not call Mignonne Fleury?" Barnabé suggested.

"How about me?" Hildegarde asked. "If I went and tickled it you-know-where do you think I'd do any more harm than La Mignonne? Anyway, how come you know what she can do with her fingers?"

In the distance Dorval could hear machines building up steam and knocking down walls, crushing bricks with a sound like rolling billiard-balls and cracking beams and making the walls whine as they resisted the blows, twisting and grinding the nails; down below there was a distant purring sound like the voices of school-children conjugating the verb "to destroy"; but Dorval knew that it would grow as loud as an earthquake: soon it would be a huge crack that would tear the City apart and move towards his house with a roar.

Madame Marchessault was at her observation post, La Vieille was in her window knitting, Barnabé Marchessault was untidily turning the pages of the notebook from his correspondence course, the Laterreur Brothers were dozing side by side, twin mountains with little girls' pouts surrounded by scars and beards; Dupont-la-France was nibbling at an apple and Cowboy was trying to build a song out of a sprinkling of words:

> When my old horse stands still
> I feed him some oats

If he wont eat his oats
I sing him the name
Of my love
Ay -ay -ay

Dorval disappeared into his apartment, then reappeared carrying two cases of beer. The stairs immediately began to tremble as the thirsty headed for the source.

"No! Go and drink with the Devil!"

Dorval placed the cases behind the bulldozer. He unscrewed the top of the gas-tank. Solemnly he poured the beer, one bottle after the other, into the giant's stomach. Then he moved back a few steps and contemplated the machine.

"As long as that bulldozer's drunk he won't think of doing any harm around here."

He went back inside. His people followed him, hoping they would be treated as well as the machine.

"Today we don't drink. We meditate."

And he hung a sign on his door and slammed it in their faces.

OUT

* * *

For several hours the impatience of the motors and the creaking of metal, a symphony of destruction, took on a growing intensity, a deeper and deeper timbre, and the choir of steel voices grew; it seemed to belong not to reality but to the echo of some dream. Dorval could not believe that such destruction was occurring in his own neighbourhood, where he had lived ever since he had decided that he had to live somewhere. They were demolishing the houses of the only people he knew in the whole world and the bulldozer was just waiting to knock down his house too. They would crumble it into dust, into fragments of brick where he had lived for more than twenty years. And yet it all seemed to him like an echo of something that was happening far away or the dream of a man who is too much alone. And that Mignonne Fleury who was running away from him. . . . Dorval drank.

"It stinks. The smell of misery is coming out of all the holes those machines are making in the walls and roofs. Rich peoples' houses must stink when they're demolished too. But they never demolish the goddam capitalists' houses."

He took another beer from the refrigerator. He felt an earthquake beneath his feet. The vibrations climbed all the way up his body, insinuating themselves like an attack of neuralgia. He raced outside.

The bulldozer still waited in its iron silence. Brown dust was falling and the sun was more beautiful than it had ever been. Towards the east the houses had already been crumbled and only bits and pieces remained. Trucks were hurrying to pick them up. They were like rats and soon they would have devoured everything. The street was filled with men who seemed to be celebrating. Dorval didn't know any of them.

"Go to hell!" he yelled at them.

"Go to hell, you goddam coffin-chasers!" from another voice that was not an echo.

Dorval looked up. In the second-floor window two big buttocks were shining out from under a raised-up skirt. Hildegarde turned around:

"I was telling them where to go . . ."

La Vieille's window opened.

"Don't make so much noise; I can't hear myself dying."

Barnabé appeared beside his wife.

"I'll never be able to study and get my mechanic's diploma with all that goddam noise. I wish it was all demolished so we wouldn't have to listen to no more noise and maybe then we'd get some peace."

"Marchessault!" Hildegarde screamed.

Dorval saw her throw something, a saucepan; a window smashed.

"Listen, you goddam savages," Dorval roared; "are you trying to demolish my house all by yourselves? I'd like to throw you all out in the street while there still is a street."

Hildegarde wiped a tear and said with a smile:

"They won't demolish us."

"*Résistance!*" Dorval proclaimed. "Everybody who wants to resist, come on down. I got beer!"

Dorval had laid in supplies for a long siege. He opened the refrigerator door and fell into his rocking-chair.

"We're at home here, us, but how about them?" (He pointed outside.) "Where's the hole they came out of? And why did they have to come here to demolish us? We aren't going to tear down their houses. Why do they come and kick us out of our own home? They must be taking orders from somebody, but who is it? Who's their Boss? Has anybody seen his face? I ain't talking about the little Bosses; them we can all recognize. They got faces like assholes. But the big Boss, it seems like they ain't got any face at all. We never see them. If they came and took a shovel-full of dirt out of the graveyard then there'd be a revolution in this country: the Bishop would shout louder than the Mayor and the Prime Minister would shout louder than all the rest. But us, we don't have the luck to be in the graveyard, we're just alive and the capitalists can take the dirt from under our boots. Isn't anybody going to open his mouth to defend the little people? You know why they don't want to open their teeth? So we can't see that they got a face full of dollars. That, *Mesdames et Messieurs*, is the key to their silence."

Baby Marchessault had fallen asleep under the table. His

little hands clutched a bottle of beer and he was chewing happily on a pacifier made of paper.

"Hildegarde!" Marchessault barked. "The kid's eating my correspondence course!"

He leaped towards the child and extirpated from him a page that had been turned into a soggy wad.

With loud cries the child demanded that it be returned. Hildegarde bent down to kiss him and Dorval's eyes caressed the pillars of her thighs that he knew were burning but capable of infinite tenderness. The Nigger was silent; his body was in the corner of the room but his soul was elsewhere.

"Only one missing is Mignonne Fleury," Dorval mused, his lips around the neck of his bottle.

"I ain't had any beer for a long time now," La Vieille complained. "I ain't dead yet but everybody's forgot about me already."

Dorval went to the refrigerator and rummaged among the stacks of bottles.

"I always seen you drinking your green tea; now at the end of your blessed life you're drinking beer like the rest of us."

"When they nail me inside my coffin it'll be too late to start then."

Dorval couldn't stop himself from lovingly embracing La Vieille and lifting her in the air.

"Dorval, after they nail me inside my coffin do you think somebody's going to go and demolish my grave?"

With even more affection Dorval pressed her to him, against his stomach, with her bottle and her knitting and all her brooches:

"I ain't got as much meat on my bones as Mignonne Fleury," she said, "but if you went and got a pump and blew me up a little you couldn't tell the difference."

A smile came to her lips that hadn't been there for a

long time, a smile that had no need of teeth.

"Ah!" Dorval exclaimed, "I love you all!"

He gave La Vieille a resounding kiss on her cheek. Cowboy intoned a hymn to love; as inspiration filled him he swelled like the Chaudière River in April.

> Love shines on my roof
> Dances in streams
> Sings through my dreams
> Like an old-fashioned king.

"Like a king, yeah, a king that hasn't got any aching bones."

"Mignonne Fleury isn't here," Dorval said sadly.

"Everybody knows how much she likes her work," Hildegarde remarked maliciously, "but this is where she ought to be, all right. She hasn't got a pension from the Government, she . . ."

Dorval spoke in his own defence.

"Me, I went to war. I SERVED THE STATE. I deserved a monument in some garden. And you, you Marchessault bitch, you should be forced to put flowers at my feet while your flabby husband takes his hat off to me."

"How about my thirteen children, aren't they a service to the State?"

"She's right," said Killer Laterreur, "the country needs people."

"He's right," Strangler agreed. "There's lots of places in Canada where you can't put on a fight because there aren't enough people to go around the ring."

"Those two keep trying, but they'll never make a baby."

"I love you, I love you all, just as though I was your own father."

They all raised their bottles to Dorval in an emotional

36

tribute to his gushing declaration. For one silent moment bottles were emptied into mouths already swollen by drunkenness. The relentless snarling of the machines passed over them like a harsh wind.

"Now that they've started," said Madame Marchessault, "they'll just keep on and never quit."

Dorval went to look out the window, then returned to his chair.

"I don't know why, but it makes me think of our boat. We were on our way to the war and we were all stuffed into tiny little compartments no bigger, well, no bigger than a coffin. There wasn't enough room for a guy to scratch his behind when it itched. If you thought about your girl that you'd left behind crying her eyes out on the shore of the St. Lawrence you'd get a hard-on that would jab your neighbour in the back! There were a few little lights here and there, almost black. We were going to fight the Germans and we were in one hell of a hurry to set foot on dry land and start fighting that war. Our knapsacks full of nice little toys that go bang were right under our feet and we were real anxious to throw them at the Germans. That's what we were all waiting for in our black holes. Not far from our boat there was something that you might call demolition going on: submarines, torpedoes, bombardiers, bombs. They were going off all around us. When the boat shook too much I'd tell myself, That's it, we're blowing up. We didn't, but it took a while before I could say, We didn't blow up.

"Yeah, there's demolition all around us, but I'm telling you, we won't blow up! We can feel the shock right through the floor; the whole neighbourhood's shaking but we aren't going to blow up. We want to go on living right here."

He looked at each of his tenants in turn, questioning them. One after another they bowed their heads or closed their eyes.

37

"When the demolition boys come here it's going to be war. Taking a man's house away is like pulling the pants off a woman. It's rape."

Beneath her flowered dress Hildegarde's thighs parted long enough for her to take a deep breath; then they closed.

They could hear the Nigger snoring in his corner of the shadow. The glutted bulldozer no longer stood in front of the door.

* * *

Men had landed like a flock of birds on the flat roofs of the buildings; they pulled off the tar-paper covers and bits of the paper went sailing through the air; nails scratched the old rust as they were pulled out and beneath the boards that crumbled to bits, the roof was so rotten, the skeletons of the houses finally appeared. Beams were thrown out the broken windows and thudded to the ground; other men who were giving hell to the workmen perched on the framework ran to pick up the fallen beams and throw them into the trucks. Higher up there were dozens of cranes armed with enormous steel balls that were suspended from chains and swaying in the wind. Here and there roofs flew abruptly into the air like enormous toads.

Dorval wandered, a stranger.

Everywhere there was the enthusiastic ardour that accompanies a man when he destroys something.

Wrecking-balls flagellated the walls which dissolved into a thick liquid of bricks and mortar. Foremen were squealing among the throbbing of the engines. Dust and dirt cried out in the axle-grease. The machines palpitated and the earth trembled beneath them: there was so much strength here, so much brute force, so much life kept boxed-in; so much power flowed through the rubber arteries that slithered along the muddy earth.

"It's a stupid life," Dorval thought, "as stupid as a cannon or a rifle. It works because it works, it works so it can go on working. It's bursting with certainty and our poor human lives limp and stammer and hesitate and it goes on for days and nights, with sickness and sleepless nights and anger and fatigue and day-dreams and other kinds of dreams too."

Walls shattered like nuts beneath the hammer-blows. The brick was fragile, like an eggshell, like the lives of men who always resemble their houses. The steel balls whistled through the air and the walls swelled up like a balloon in a net. Dust from the cement stuck to sweat and fell into eyes. The beams and pillars that were still standing looked like broken bones. Time had welded these pieces together like the branch to the trunk. Bulldozers made smoking piles of the débris that was impregnated with all the odours of humanity.

"Life stinks just like death."

The odour of men and women, the odour of tears and fatigue, the odour of quarrels and neuroses, the odour of boiled potatoes and of work; the wood and brick had taken on the odour of the people who lived in them like clothing on skin, but the bulldozers were aware of nothing, nor were the new cranes that chewed at the débris with their oversized teeth.

Everything was clean. The engines were silent, the machines were still. Still boiling with frenzy they left the place, their operators thinking of their haggard wives and whining children.

The dead clay where marks of tires and tracks were engraved had no memory of any life. The people Dorval had known, all those he had not known and those who had lived in the neighbourhood before him, all these families and all these generations had been buried under the blows of shovels and cranes and bulldozers, with no funerals or wreaths or tears. To look at the overturned ground Dorval was walking

39

on, one would never think they had even lived.

"It's worse than war—we don't even hate each other."

One day Dorval would be destroyed too. The ship that was the City drifted through the night with all its windows illuminated. He was in a hole with no light; he felt he was in the skin of a black man, he felt so much like a stranger on this earth. He could have gone back towards the City but he just wanted to stay at the bottom of the huge gap the machines had made in his life.

"We dream of conquering the moon, that frosty old lady that gives you head-colds. And why do we do it? Because the earth is uninhabitable."

A force that was imprisoned in his chest sighed like an ox. A sea had been awakened in him: waves, foam, tides, surf. He stretched out his arms in the solitary night of his eradicated neighbourhood. He would resist. Dorval was the king of this domain. Raising his eyes defiantly to Heaven he became aware of the moon. His body, a little bit drunk from beer and a little bit drunk from sorrow, but drunk most of all from life itself, was shaken by a profound shudder and a great laugh burst out like a flash of lightning: it had just occurred to Dorval that his penis wanted to let go and hurl itself in an immense explosion, raising the dust from the ruins of the neighbourhood and rising up towards the planet in the midst of the night, which would open welcoming legs to it.

"The moon isn't any farther away than Mignonne Fleury."

All had been undermined. The houses he had looked at in the morning now existed only in his memory. Here and there some bricks had been forgotten. Dorval picked up a few, made a pile of them, a little wall, went to look for more and began to build a house, attentive as a child to his labours. Completely absorbed by the game he adjusted, re-arranged, propped up walls; he made a door, windows, began to build a second storey, aligned the windows. The neighbourhood had been cleaned out the way a table is cleared after a meal. But they wouldn't demolish Dorval! He would fight. *Résistance! Résistance!* This rotten capitalist City deserved a good lashing. He knocked down all the capitalists with one good solid kick; but he also knocked over his little brick house. When he put his foot down to continue his walk he felt a pain as though an invisible bulldozer had smashed his toes. Dorval hopped on one foot to the Hôtel-Dieu Hospital and went home in a taxi, like a king, his foot encased in white plaster.

"There's no God," he told Hildegarde who had come to the window to see whose car was stopping in front of the house, "but I pray that he'll make all the goddam capitalists suffer as much as I'm suffering."

* * *

Dorval's door shook with nervous authority. He leaped out of bed. By the colour of the light he judged that it was very early. He opened the door, pouring out curses accumulated during a night when sleep had been impossible. A small man baked by the sun, wearing overalls that were too big for him, stood before Dorval:

"Excuse me, I come to demolish you."

"Baby Jesus' holy bum, if you lay a hand on my house it'll be over my dead body."

Behind the little man was a yellow demolition machine, all its parts humming, its arm, suspended over the roof, containing thunder.

"Goddam capitalist slave!"

Dorval realized that he was naked.

"Look, Hairless, I ain't ready to go out yet."

His arm encircled the shoulder of the little man who, uncomfortable against this nudity, felt himself drawn inside,

41

then dragged to Dorval's apartment and led to the re-frigerator full of beer. Dorval tossed a bottle at the man's stomach.

"Hey, it's too early to start drinking!"

"But not too early to come and knock down the house of an honest man, an honest tax-payer, not to mention a war-hero! Goddam slave! You think drinking a beer's a crime, but kicking me out on the street like a whore in her bed, that you could do easier than rhyming off a prayer to baby Jesus!"

Dorval went into his bedroom and put on his yellow-and-green striped undershorts.

"What's wrong with a guy doing his work?"

"You got the mentality of a slave; it'll never change either, it's like the colour of your skin. If your boss asked you to scrub his ass with your toothbrush you'd do it with your tongue, you're so keen."

Hairless wanted to get out but he was paralyzed with bewilderment. Chest and feet bare, bottle in hand, Dorval sat down in his chair.

"Look here, you capitalist slave, there's still one man in this hell of a life on earth that's got the right to drink his bottle of beer when he wants to and he can drink as much as he wants too. That's me, that man. You ought to stand at attention when you look at me. I'm a war hero too."

Hairless was open-mouthed, incredulous.

"Look at my certificate of honour on the wall."

The little man went over to the wall, his eyes glued to the document. After a moment, he said:

"I can talk English but I don't know how to read it too good."

"That ain't English, it's French like you and me! But I hung up my certificate upside down to insult the army."

Hairless moved back towards the door, smiling politely:

42

"I gotta start my work."

"You ain't even pissed the beer I gave you and you're talking about putting a hole in my roof."

"I'd rather work in construction but there isn't none; the banks are as poor as Job. There ain't no jobs in construction. The future's in demolition."

"This isn't the war. Me, I haven't declared war on nobody. There isn't a single goddam capitalist on the face of this earth or anywhere else that's got the right to tear the guts out of my house. My house belongs to me, just like my skin."

"That's progress for you; that's how things work nowadays."

Dorval dropped his bottle of beer and waved his rocking-chair at Hairless, who turned pale.

"Blind goddam slave!" he thundered. "Progress! Progress! We'll have progress when you let an honest man live in peace in his own house."

Dorval coughed so that he could go on talking. The muscles of his neck were knotted in anger. He put down the chair.

"There'll be progress when guys like you and guys like me go off hand in hand to demolish the rich guys' houses."

Hairless lacked the strength to drink.

"You don't haveta demolish the rich guys' houses; they're all nice and clean and pretty, with good taste."

"Painted with the sweat of the poor like you and me."

Hairless was turning from white to green:

"You wouldn't be a communist, would you?"

He looked at Dorval with horror.

"Yeah, I'm a communist. A real one. Like you're a real capitalist. The only difference is that I'm not gonna demolish your house."

Dorval held out a bottle to Hairless.

"A communist," he repeated, "and a great war hero."

Dorval began to rock. His chair, with its oscillating movements, was a boat climbing in his memory up the waves of time.

"Once it was dark," Dorval began. "Dark like a capitalist's soul. We were in a plane. To get over being scared we were telling the dirtiest stories we could think of but nobody felt like laughing. It was like our mouths were constipated. We wanted to bawl. If somebody had got the bright idea of telling one of the fairy-tales we used to hear when we were kids we would have cried hard enough to need umbrellas. All of a sudden I felt something hit me in the back. But instead of landing with my face on the floor I realized my four paws were dangling in the air, at the end of the cords of my parachute. If you want to try to understand what I felt like, imagine yourself falling out of the two-thousandth floor of a building. It smelled good, the brand new night. I fell lower and lower. Tweet! Tweet! just like a little bird except I couldn't climb back up again. I was scared, *Sainte Vierge!* I was dying with fright. I told myself, if I can keep my both eyes open I won't die. Somebody told me there'd be places you could take your bearing from but there wasn't anything under me except a big black cloud—the earth. Me, I like it here on earth. That's what they made me out of and when I die that's what I'll go back to. And when I was out there hanging from the ends of my parachute cords, still alive, I was pretty anxious to get down to earth, feel it under my feet and stick my nose in it like a kid sticks his nose in his mother's belly when he comes home from school. Then all of a sudden I felt something sort of like a kick in the ass. Good old Mother Earth welcoming me back home. I fell down, rolled around, flattened out. I wasn't landing on the ground, the ground was jumping up on top of me and smashing me. I was dead; my eyes were shut."

Hairless was listening with his mouth agape, clinging to his bottle of beer as though he were shipwrecked and it was a buoy.

"I was scared to death but I could hear the leaves whispering around me. It was the wind—or maybe it wasn't.

"I saw a black shape coming towards me. It was climbing, coming closer. They'd told us to be careful because there'd be more Germans than French waiting for us.

" 'Here.'

"The shape was whispering in French. First I thought it was a girl. Then I remembered that all the Frenchmen talk like girls. I slid through the grass towards the voice. As I was moving I could feel my whole body getting warm. I dragged myself closer to the voice and the heat got even hotter. Then all of a sudden I could see the voice: it was a girl! At a time like that when you think your life's over because your heart's stopped beating and then all of a sudden, pow! it starts all over again and your heart dances from head to toe, what does it mean?

" 'I came to ask you to marry me, Mamzelle.' "

Dorval had stopped rocking. He looked around him, squinting. As he spoke, images from the past were projected onto the wall.

"The voice answered: 'I'm married to my country'."

Dorval looked down at the pitiful little bald man to whom it was forbidden to understand the true meaning of such a declaration. Hairless avoided Dorval's triumphant look: now he envied him. He had never experienced such romantic adventures. His Isidorina lived in the house opposite him: when he married her he had simply crossed the street. For a moment the adventures he had never had quivered in the depths of his pale eyes.

"I understood what she meant right away," Dorval continued. "And I was ashamed, so ashamed I wanted to vomit. Can you understand why I was so ashamed?"

Hairless was still dreaming about what he had never known.

"While there were some men who had less respect for other men than they had for their own shit, while men were killing other men with rifles because they were too civilized to eat them like cannibals, while men were dancing a dance of death around a fire—not a wood fire like the Indians make, but a nice civilized fire started by a bomb—while the night was thick and the earth was indifferent as though there weren't any men on its back," (Dorval wiped away a tear with his fingertip, ashamed to be crying like a woman), "while men were afraid that this war was getting worse and worse, wrecking the earth, while men and women were mourning over their homelands as though they were at a wake, while the Germans were making leather pants for their whores out of the skins of Jews, can you imagine, Hairless, can you just imagine me saying to the little girl that came to watch me land with my parachute, 'I come to ask you to marry me'? I'm still ashamed of it thirty years later. I'm ashamed. *Sainte Vierge*, I'm ashamed. I'd like to climb back into my mother's belly, start my life all over. Maybe not be so stupid.

"I wasn't very proud of myself, but how about you, Hairless? You go around destroying buildings so how can you understand it? I should have cried all the tears I had inside me but I would have needed a bucket the size of the Prime Minister's swimming-pool. I didn't cry. There was just one idea plugged into my brain: to screw that perfumed little pearl that had come to me out of the night. A nice way to get your passport stamped, eh? I'm ashamed. When you want to make love it's a sign of life: it's something a dead man doesn't think about much. But in the exceptional circumstances of that night in the middle of a world war I was sorry

I'd wanted to do that particular kind of Québécois tap-dance. And I still feel sorry about it today.

"But she wasn't discouraged by my gross stupidity and the little soldier came and clung to me. There was courage crackling like fire in that little body of hers. She'd come all by herself, at night, when the wolves were howling with German accents. Yes, *Monsieur*, I'm telling you the truth.

" 'Excuse me, Mamzelle, sometimes I'm too eager for it. You could say that I'm bursting with health.'

"That's how I tried to apologize.

" 'Where do you come from?' she asked me.

" 'From the airplane, Mamzelle.'

" 'Your accent! It's dreadful!'

" 'I come from Canada, Mamzelle. They paid for my fare and our accent don't kill nobody!'

" 'When they hear that accent they know that help is coming. My name is Jeanne.'

"So me that's been talking French like we talk it in Canada, I learned to talk it like the Frenchmen. The men over there, when they talk they sound like they got a candy stuck to their tongue. But when you hear the women, *hostie* that sounds pretty, prettier than a bird that sings to you every morning from the branch on the tree outside your window, sitting under his leaf all wet with dew . . . And you, you go around destroying houses so you can't have any idea about what makes things beautiful.

"Anyway, I disguised myself, passed myself off for some anonymous Frenchman. I had grammar to eat three times a day, I pinched my lips, I sharpened the tip of my tongue, I oiled the hinges of my jaws and in two weeks I was talking French as good as General de Gaulle's own brother. Yeah—I forgot a little since but I swear if a German turned up in here right now I'd start in talking again just like a real Frenchman. Well, Hairless, here we are. You destroy houses.

47

You wouldn't be a Nazi in disguise, would you? They exist, you know."

Hairless turned red.

"*Christ!* you don't have to insult me like that."

He threw his bottle of beer which bounced back out of the corner. Then, shaking and white with rage and looking as though he wanted to tear out his heart and throw it at Dorval's head like a stone:

"Not another word out of you. You know I'm not alone. I got a bulldozer behind me and behind the bulldozer there's the government."

"Don't get so worked up. You got a big machine, me I got a big head. Hairless, it isn't you that's going to decide if the rich guys' big machine is stronger than one poor man's big head."

Soothed by Dorval's voice and the calmness of his manner, Hairless picked up another bottle of beer. Dorval shouted towards the ceiling:

"Dupont!"

He waited, his eyes raised as though the person he had called might descend from the ceiling.

"Dupont!" Dorval repeated, more insistently.

Footsteps could be heard running down the stairs; beret on his head, chest bare, Dupont appeared.

"Dupont-la-France," Dorval ordered, "talk French to this here gentleman."

"To begin with, I refuse, I absolutely refuse to speak to some stranger if one does not have the courtesy to introduce him to me formally. Next, I really have nothing to say to this gentleman. And finally, I do dislike having my moments of reflection disturbed to suit your whims and fancy."

Baldy watched with amazement the agility of the moustache-covered mouth.

"You hear that, Hairless? That's the way I used to talk."

48

Dorval rose to salute the passing of his youth.

"It was Jeanne-la-Pucelle, you know, that's what they call Joan of Arc over in France, Joan the Virgin, anyway she's the one that taught me how to talk her language. She taught me how to write too. Oh, I could really write in those days. I ain't a goddam illiterate like you that don't know nothing except how to knock down the houses our fathers built with their own hands. But I used to write the way you walk: with a limp. My letters were all crooked, like your soul. Here, have a beer. Jeanne told me, 'Your calligraphy'—calligraphy, you get that? No? It's a fish that swims backwards so it won't get water in its eyes—'your calligraphy,' Jeanne told me, 'is as frightful as your accent. Your writing is hesitant, tortuous. Your letters are awkward. The collaborators will recognize that your calligraphy isn't French. The Germans will interrogate you. And since you have an accent like a Canadian Indian . . .'

"Then Jeanne-la-Pucelle took my hand and helped me write my letters and my hand in her little hand followed her just like a child. You, Hairless, you can't imagine how soft the hand of a daughter of France is. Warm, too. An angel's hand wouldn't be as smooth as hers. I'll tell you something. A French girl's little hand is softer than any of the goddam handles on your demolition machine. But while my right hand was learning how to write words in a school-kid's scribbler the other one wanted to play games under La Pucelle's skirt.

"But she kept saying, 'No! we're fighting a war. After France is liberated there will be the Revolution. All the French people will be happy, we'll all take off our clothes and make love. Then I may think again of a Canadian who came out of the sky in a parachute.'

"Look at me, Hairless. Why are you trying to demolish the house of a man that's heard such pretty talk?

"The night I made my parachute jump La Pucelle took me to a stable that was hidden under the trees: plane-trees they called them. In the stable there was hay and horse-shit and they smell the same everywhere, but there was also a bunch of men from the village, some women too but mostly men that were married and had families. They were soldiers at night and in the morning they went back home to get dressed up like butchers and bakers and waiters and road-workers—if the Germans didn't get to them first. You can believe me or not, whatever you want, but every one of them was a communist."

"Communists!" Hairless, dozing because of the beer and the length of the story, woke up suddenly. "Communists!"

"*Oui, monsieur*, communists. Those men were patriots and they hadn't kept their eyes shut for the last few years.

"Jeanne-la-Pucelle used to ride her bicycle to the next village every evening. I never knew what she went there for. One night she didn't come back. There's no God but I prayed to him anyway, asked him to let her go on taking her bicycle rides for a long time."

The first few times he told this story Dorval had wept; now he had told it so often he no longer wept. But he was still just as sad.

"Hey, that girl, that Pouzelle, was she one of them communists too?"

Dorval covered himself with pride.

"She was a communist just like me."

Hairless exploded with anger. He smashed his bottle against a wall, his shouts flew through the air and he had already leaped onto his machine.

"*Tabernacle de communiste de crucifix*, I'm gonna smash this house of yours to powder before you poison the whole neighbourhood."

The demolition machine roared with all its power. Bang!

Zing! Bang! Bullets clanked against the steel. Bang! Zing! Dorval pointed his rifle at Hairless who was running backwards.

"To hell with you! I opened my heart to you and all you do is shit in it! Goddam Hairless, don't turn your rear-end in my direction if you don't want a bullet to make you another ass-hole."

Bang! Zing! The bullets continued to clank against the machine. Baldy took off, confessing his sins to God. Bang! Zing! A bullet whistled past him, so close he could feel its heat biting into his skull. He flung himself behind a pile of bricks. Bang! Zip! A bullet sank into the brick.

Dorval was the greatest hero in America. *Résistance!*

La Vieille stood in her window, applauding him. Mignonne Fleury was standing at her window too:

"He could do his resisting with a little less banging around, Dorval. Think of the working men!"

She moved away, called back by a voice from her bed.

"Résistance! Résistance!" the thirteen Marchessault children chanted, dancing around Dorval.

"I'll protect the whole lot of you just like as if I was your own father."

Dorval kissed his rifle, which was still warm. Dupont-la-France approached him.

"Do drink this glass of apple-juice. You must be strong if you are to resist. Apples contain powers, because they take all the best things from the earth."

* * *

Rifle in hand, Dorval stood guard all day long. He awaited the return of the demolition crew from a perch on one of the Marchessaults' windows.

A few days before, children had been howling and

squabbling on every floor of all the surrounding houses; their fat mothers were silent, exhausted; they would break out suddenly into animal cries and then fall silent once again.

"A man's life isn't worth a fart," said Dorval.

"Don't talk dirty in front of my kids that I'm trying to bring up like Christians," said Hildegarde.

She pulled the diaper off a whining child. Dorval watched her breasts swing back and forth inside her dress. Marchessault, lying over his motor, was trying to loosen a screw.

"Wait till I'm finished my correspondence course; life's gonna be different."

"I'm telling you," said Dorval, "there's always gonna be a bigger motor that you won't know how to fix."

Hildegarde interrupted. "Me, I think he'll be dead before he's done that course."

Dorval didn't take his eyes off her pendulous breasts as she bent maternally over the child.

"Even love," said Dorval, "even a great love is wind, less than wind. We don't need machines to demolish love. You just have to leave it to time."

Dorval was looking at the patch of ground where death had been spread out by the bulldozers. He wasn't thinking now of Hildegarde's breasts but of a mowing machine, an old mowing machine pulled by horses through the green fields of his childhood with the rattling sound of gears, often in need of oiling, that could be heard from far away in the silence that was so beautiful, like pure water. Huge quantities of grass fell down. Its strong scent made him cough. Sometimes it even gave him a nosebleed.

He looked over the destruction machine that Hairless had abandoned under the whistling threat of the bullets.

Hairless returned. He was not alone. A priest in a black soutane followed him, his white surplice gleaming.

"I bring you peace," the man of God announced from a distance.

"Peace? That I had before you got here."

Dorval bent his head slightly.

"Excuse me, *Monsieur le Curé*, but as long as you've got your altar boy with you I ain't entitled to be polite."

"Are you the one that's the communist?" the priest asked with a smile.

"Are you the last Catholic on the island of Montreal?" Dorval replied.

Hairless gave the young priest the holy-water basin that was hidden behind his back; the priest took a sprinkler that had been concealed in his pocket ready for use, and began to sprinkle Dorval with holy-water. What power did the rifle have against such a weapon?

"Don't drown me, *Monsieur le Curé*."

Dorval was laughing, his mouth a slit. The priest was speaking Latin, which worried him a little. *"Vade retro Satanas."*

"I'm sending the Devil away. Satan, leave the soul of my son."

The word was more insulting to Dorval than a slap.

"I ain't your son and when I was a baby it wasn't holy-water I sucked, it was real milk out of the real tits of a real woman."

"Leave, Satan, *fugite Satanas*, the soul of this man, *illi hominis animum!*"

Dorval turned red. Anger spread through his arteries and his muscles trembled.

"Watch out. I can feel the Devil leaving me. He's getting out, *Monsieur le Curé*. Don't you see him? He's going. He's coming. You'd better leave."

Holy-water was raining down on him. Dorval trembled in a dance that grew more frenetic; his face turned redder and he sweated, jumped, twirled his rifle, waved his fist, gesticulated, became more excited, and began to bay like a hound. Hairless gradually moved away from him.

"The Devil's leaving, he's leaving, I can see him."

Dorval's dance became madder and more vehement; he whirled around, sweat pouring off him; his belly shook and he roared.

"Leave me, Satan!"

Dorval instantly stopped moving.

"He's gone now. Thanks, *Monsieur le Curé*. You helped me hatch my devil."

The priest said,

"Let us give thanks to all-powerful God who rules over Heaven and earth."

A shot. Another. Bang.

"Now my devil's out he wants to give you a good kick in the ass!"

Hairless was already far away. Bang! The priest, his soutane raised to his neck, was running as fast as his feet would carry him; he was so white that even his soutane looked pale. Dorval was behind him, exhausted and panting, shooting invisible bullets at the sky. As long as he lived the young priest would claim that the Devil exists because he had seen him with his own eyes. Bang! Dorval stopped to allow himself the pleasure of seeing them run. Bang! The priest and Hairless had Satan's claws in their behinds.

Dorval walked back slowly through the demolished neighbourhood. He kissed the barrel of his rifle. What a lovely war! In all the time he had been a soldier this was his proudest moment. He was smiling. Beneath this overturned earth, these crumbled bricks, beneath all this débris a heart was beating. It seemed to him that green plants were already growing, wiping out the destruction as joy erases an old sorrow.

The children were lying on the ground, bored. The noisy machines, the buildings that burst like balloons, had been like a party for them. Now it was all finished. The party would not begin again until the machines came back to attack their house, Dorval's house.

"What are you kids doing?"

"We're bored," a whining child replied.

"Goddam cursed little brats, you got to tear down the whole city to make them happy."

"Are we moving today?" Hildegarde teased.

She was leaning out the window, laughing, but Dorval could see nothing but the marvellous bodice, her twin jewels shimmering in its shadow. Behind her, Marchessault was cursing as he hammered at his motor.

"When it's all demolished," said La Vieille, "it's going to look real pretty, like the countryside at Sainte-Sabine-de-Bellechasse where my late husband took me after our wedding. We'll be able to see the sky."

She sighed as she uttered the last word.

"The capitalists have bought the sky," Dorval replied. "They surveyed it and sold it back to other capitalists."

La Vieille's knitting was hanging out the window and her eyes were lost in a dream that stretched out far above the black tarred roofs, the twisted walls and winding stairs. Despite the years, after an entire lifetime, Montreal was as far away as it had been when La Vieille had first left Sainte-Sabine-de-Bellechasse. That was what she was dreaming of now behind eyes that gazed at the citadel dominating the city. Dorval, too, was dreaming as he looked at the City before him.

"The capitalists' skyscrapers look like giant's legs."

Madame Marchessault giggled as though he had said something obscene.

"Look. The capitalists' buildings are legs and feet. The head? We can't see it. The head of capitalism is invisible. It's like God. Take a good look, because those big legs are going to move, the big feet are going to rise, slip a bit; you're going to see their big soles because you'll be underneath them. The army of skyscrapers is going to descend: look at them, stamping their feet already. They're trembling at the smell of open terrain. They've been sneering ever since they saw the first buildings come down."

And with a gesture that restored to him all the warrior's conviction he had possessed as a soldier, Dorval pointed his rifle at the gray giants and opened fire.

"*Résistance!*" shouted La Vieille.

"At your age you won't resist very long," said Madame Marchessault.

* * *

The destroying engine, fixed in all the patience of its steel, was waiting for the order to attack. Cowboy whistled, imitating the sound of the wind riding through the prairie grass; the Nigger was sleeping. Dorval was the sole guardian of his house. Alone, he waited. Dazed by the noonday sun, he leaned against the door-frame and put the butt of his rifle on the ground so that the barrel rubbed against his pant-leg and he dreamed of a woman's hand on his thigh. He shuddered in his torpor.

"That Mignonne Fleury! Where is she? Stirring up a storm in some capitalist's pants most likely. Instead of helping me with the Resistance. If the circumstances were the same Jeanne-la-Pucelle would be here beside me. She'd be the one with the rifle in her hands. Jeanne-la-Pucelle wouldn't leave me alone against the whole universe. Good God! Good God! that round little ass of hers, that thin waist and the rest of her body that flared out like an expensive vase, overflowing. I mean she was so nice and round, everywhere she was supposed to be. Good God! But during the war when she was with the Resistance that little wildflower was as strong as any bulldozer. I can still see her on her bicycle. The seat came right up between her cheeks. When she pedalled, the wind would lift up her skirt and play, yeah, right there where you're thinking. She looked as if she was in a parachute, little Jeanne-la-Pucelle. She'd told me to meet her on the terrace of the Cheval Blanc, I remember. She said, 'Whatever happens, you don't know me, you've never seen me.' It was a beautiful sunny day and I was drinking my beer, looking at an old church and thinking it was older than the oldest thing I knew in Canada. I saw Jeanne coming, her skirt tucked up, the sun shining between her thighs. *Messieurs!* She was pedalling and then she came up next to a man and braked with her foot. It slid on the pavingstones, she pulled her skirt down over her knees and whack! she slapped that man in the face with one hand and then whack! she slapped him again with the other one.

" 'Filthy swine!' she yelled. That's a fancy way they got in France to call somebody a goddam pig.

"Then wham! she hit him in the face again. Me, I didn't know her, but I was on my feet. Three other guys on bicycles turned up all of a sudden, coming out from behind the plane-trees. They jumped on the man and started to pound him a little harder. The guy's face was red with blood and his tongue was hanging out his nose. Nobody there knew who he was neither. The men that were protecting La Pucelle were kicking him and his head was bouncing around like a soccer ball. Jeanne had disappeared. I saw her again that evening.

" 'What was all that about?' I asked her in my brand-new accent that I'd borrowed for the war.

The angel put her finger to her lips:

" '*Résistance.*'

"The guy they'd just put through the meat-grinder worked for the police and he'd pulled our friends' ears a bit too hard during an interrogation in another town a few miles away. Jeanne, what a woman! She had more courage in her little boobs than there was in the whole French army. She wasn't always thinking about her ass like Mignonne Fleury. If Jeanne found herself in front of a demolition machine like the one in front of my house she'd jump on it like it was her bicycle, she'd start it up and then she'd go knock down a capitalist bank. But Mignonne Fleury . . ."

In fact Mignonne Fleury was just arriving on the arm of a man Dorval recognized immediately, and with fury: Hairless, the operator of the demolition machine.

"You skinny little fart, so you got the nerve to show your face around here again, eh? I'll show you the way back home!"

Mignonne stepped between them. Dorval, his face contorted by the good sensations he had just experienced, opened the door to leave the way clear. Mignonne went in, followed by Hairless. They disappeared up the stairs, Hairless stumbling at every step.

When he came back in a few minutes, his eyes veiled with pleasure and too full of ecstasy to be able to bear the light of day as well, his legs quivering as though he were drunk, Hairless climbed onto his machine; it turned its back on Dorval's house and drove away, backfiring. Mignonne Fleury buttoned up her dress, saying,

"*Résistance!*"

* * *

In the thick evening air the wind raised clumps of ashy dust as though fire had played some part in the destruction; it also revealed an odour of urine. Nothing else was left.

Dorval took a few steps. The cast on his foot slipped on a brick. He picked it up and threw it at the face of the night. It fell to earth, breaking to pieces as it struck against the other débris.

"You don't throw very far, Dorval. Your muscles are all gone soft!"

Mignonne Fleury was teasing. Dorval did not reply but he turned around, waiting for her. She approached him slowly. Dorval thought, "She wants me to want her to be here."

"It's horrible," she said.

"What?"

"All those houses, just gone."

"Life's horrible."

Mignonne Fleury walked close beside him; her female warmth spread over his shoulders.

"People live in a goddam garbage-can," he said.

Mignonne Fleury's hand clasped his wrist, like a chain that was far too gentle.

"Listen," Mignonne whispered.

Silently Dorval moved closer to her; he put his arm next to hers and clenched his fist to tighten the muscles in his wrist. He wanted Mignonne's hand to feel the strength that was quivering through him. He also wanted to feel more intimately the motionless caress of Mignonne's hand on his arm. Above them the city was trembling in a nervous scintillation. There was nothing around them but the silence of what had been demolished.

"If we don't look at the City it's as if we were all alone on the earth."

"Mignonne Fleury, I'm hungry for you and I'm thirsty for you too."

She burst out in a laugh that went all the way up to Sainte-Catherine Street.

"Come on."

She dragged him along and the débris of brick and gravel sounded beneath their feet. Suddenly they tripped. Somebody was lying on the ground.

"*Sainte Vierge*, leave us alone!"

It was the voice of Hildegarde Marchessault in the darkness.

"For Heaven's sake, can't they leave us in peace?" sighed Dupont-la-France.

Choked with laughter, Mignonne and Dorval left the nocturnal love-nest and moved towards a stripped, bare wall that was still standing. He struck a match and moved it around.

"It used to be a bedroom: there's still some wallpaper."

Dorval threw the match away and took Mignonne in his arms. She let her head fall onto his shoulder and whispered in his ear:

"You aren't getting me, Dorval; you aren't."

He tightened his embrace and she bit his shoulder gently.

"Listen," she said.

He listened carefully. Someone was breathing hard behind the wall. They both listened. The breathing became tortured. An impatient voice said,

"Marchessault, are you still there?"

The breathing behind the wall became even more intense.

"Marchessault, your wife's right. You're no better on a woman than you are on that motor."

"It's La Vieille!" Dorval exclaimed.

He laughed so hard that his arms opened, but Mignonne still clung to him.

"You aren't getting me, Dorval," she teased, laughing.

He embraced her again.

Beneath the profound night, like the mystery of God who doesn't exist, the demolished neighbourhood sighed with love as it had when there still were curtains on the windows. The Nigger had left his room and ventured as far as the front door; naked, he was adoring the silence and the night.

"The earth, ah! what a bordello!" Dorval repeated. "What a bordello of a bordello!"

"If that's all you can say to a woman I'm leaving; you aren't getting me, Dorval!"

She pulled Dorval's hands off her breasts and ran away in the night.

Cowboy, sitting on a stack of piled-up beams, was scrutinizing the sky with the eyes of a Western movie-star. He stood up. With the ungainly walk of a prairie man he walked up towards the City, tossing crumbs of music:

> Night is a tree
> That grows in my heart
> And I tie up my horse

"That goddam Cowboy is going to make me scream," said Strangler Laterreur.

And he buried his head in the hollow of Killer's shoulder; an enormous tear was dropping from his eye.

* * *

Dorval's house was still standing, on earth that was dead and without memory. Hands behind his back, he walked about with the majesty of a king contemplating his own monument.

"I won my war all by myself!"

Mignonne appeared; he ran. She fled. He caught her. The beautiful fruits that his hands had stroked with so much pleasure the night before trembled in her décolletage. She released herself.

"You aren't getting me, Dorval."

Dorval tried again to imprison Mignonne's waist in his arms. She pushed his hand away, but she listened to him.

"Mignonne Fleury, if you want we could let the grass

grow all around my house as thick as a capitalist's rug. Then you and I could walk barefoot on it. When we walked we'd feel the earth under our feet."

Mignonne Fleury turned her back on Dorval's speech.

"I still have to earn my living while I'm waiting for you to turn the city into the back forty. Now they've demolished everything I got no more market. I got to export myself."

She was already gone.

"If you wanted to you'd figure out how to earn your living here," he hesitated; "honourably."

Her behind wiggled with an insidious impudence. Dorval felt the earth moving under his feet with the same rhythm.

"Mignonne!" he called. "We'll make a vegetable garden: we'll plant tomatoes and celery and leeks and make organic soups."

"We can plant turnips too, turnips like you!"

She disappeared into an alley at the edge of the demolished neighbourhood. But Dorval could still hear her laughter.

He came to tell his tenants of his plan to cultivate the earth.

"We're still here. The house is still standing. The capitalists are going to try to take the earth away from under our feet. In these grave circumstances"—here, he climbed up onto his chair so that like the chief of a tribe he could be above his entourage, especially those great cows the Laterreur Brothers—"at this grave moment I say that we must sow before we can reap. The seeds will mark our names on what belongs to us."

"First of all, most urgently, we must plant apple-trees," said Dupont-la-France. "Plant apples where slums used to stand: that will be the real Revolution!"

"Adam's apple was man's first sin," said Hildegarde; "now Dupont's apple's going to save us."

"As long as I can still bite into an apple nobody's got the right to nail me in my coffin."

Cowboy, sitting in the window, scratched a few chords on his guitar:

> Look at my horses
> Fly through the fields
> Like sleek white ships

After a long sunny afternoon the dazzling day began to fall asleep over the city. Dorval, the Marchessaults and their flock of children, La Vieille, Dupont-la-France, the Laterreur Brothers and Cowboy were crouched over the earth, moving like sun-baked peasants. They scrabbled in the ground with knives, forks, nails, screw-drivers, broom-handles. Their ploughing had to be done before the sun had disappeared behind the skyscrapers. The earth was waking up after so many years of uselessness. Clothed in the last rays of the sun, Dorval threw seeds which were scattered by the breeze. The day was completely extinguished. Then the Nigger came out of his room and stood in the door to watch the planters' shadows. In a regal voice, Dorval commanded:

"Let the rain fall!"

Just as regally he opened his fly and copiously watered the patches he had planted. In his belly he felt the happiness of God creating vegetation on the earth. His people listened piously to the rain. Then all the other men copied him. The women were silent and the contemplative earth listened to the music of men overflowing with the joy of having accomplished a great feat.

"Everybody back to my place," Dorval ordered. "You've earned your beer!"

The Nigger went back into his room.

"The beer will be warm," said Dorval. "The goddam

63

capitalists cut off the power. They'd take away the air we breathe if they could."

He took an old kerosene lantern out from under the sink. There was light. He distributed the bottles. The children weren't neglected either, because they were just as thirsty as the adults; their throats were dry from the dust. Bottle-caps flew off and beer flowed into sweating bellies. Peace reigned, like the green and perfumed peace you find beneath a tree sated with rain. Marchessault was worried. He hadn't even put his bottle to his mouth.

"Me, I lost a whole day," he moaned. "I shoulda been spending that time on my motor. Every day I lose puts me back a day. I been losing days that put me back a day for years now."

"Hildegarde Marchessault," said Dorval, "you should get down on your knees before a man like Barnabé." Her reply was a sneer.

"Marchessault, don't look so glum. I'm going to tell you about one of my adventures."

Before following Dorval on the reckless road of his biography they took the precaution of swallowing a good mouthful of beer. Dorval wiped his lips with the back of his hand and began:

"It was during the war, the time of Jeanne-la-Pucelle."

"I'd sure like to know if she really deserved that name Pucelle," Hildegarde said, her laugh drowning in the foaming beer that spread over her chin and her breast.

"You must have been pretty young yourself when you lost it, Madame Marchessault. Can you even remember what the word means?"

Sitting on the table or crushed on the floor among the scattered bottles, Dorval's tenants were contorted with laughter. They wiped the tears off their faces with hands that were blackened by the earth they had ploughed with their improvised tools. The mixture of sweat and dust turned to mud. Dorval reigned from his rocking-chair. To announce that he was going to speak again he raised his bottle and extended a papal arm. The laughter diminished and the lantern-light on their faces became less febrile.

"If a man sleeps well and eats well and his intestines feel like being cleaned out at least once a day I say there's a happy man. After my parachute landing in the occupied zone the Frenchmen hid me in a cave. I didn't have the right to open my mouth because they were scared my accent would keep Hitler awake. I had to grow a big mustache like the Frenchmen too. They made me eat lettuce and water-cress and asparagus and spinach: rabbit-food. I learned a different way to say all the words I knew, even the ones I learned at my mother's knee. Jeanne-La-Pucelle was the one that taught me now to talk. When I said my word properly sometimes she'd sort of tickle my back, scratch it like a cat: then I'd feel something spring in me that went zing! and wanted to send me to the moon. But La Pucelle wouldn't let me lay a finger on her. Good Lord, I felt like I was at death's door. Imagine a fire that's burning but hasn't got a nice fat log to burn up. But I guess I was happy because I slept all night without any bad dreams, my appetite was good, so good the Frenchmen started putting a couple of potatoes in with the rabbit food they gave me; and at least once a day my bottom opened up like the locks at Saint-Lambert. Time passed, but I wasn't shaken up; and it passed for the others too. I was happy to be alive on French soil. In the midst of my happiness it was a toilet-bowl that got me started reading. I'd bolt the door of the crapper and to kill time I started reading the roll of toilet-paper. Maybe France is guilty of inventing handles for coffee-cups to give them an excuse for sticking their little fingers out in the air, but they weren't the ones that invented toilet-paper with flowers and little birds on it. Not them.

They collected newspapers and cut them into squares. When I was fighting the war I'd read the toilet-paper: one sheet, two sheets, three . . . In the end I didn't even dare to wipe myself because it didn't seem like the right thing to do with all those fine ideas. I often went to the crapper just for the pleasure of reading. It was more than a pleasure: it was a thirst, a thirst *messieurs!* I even used to steal the toilet-paper. I'd hide it in my sleeves and my socks; I was so hungry and thirsty in my room; I'd pick up all the pieces and try to put the page together again. But often they were full of holes. So I'd read around the hole. Toilet-paper was my library; the toilet, *Monsieur le Ministre de l'éducation*, was my university."

* * *

There was a spattering of applause. Bottles rolled across the floor. Dorval opened another case. The Marchessault children threaded through the adults' legs, arguing over the bottles. Bottlecaps went flying. Dorval threw a bottle to the end of the hallway and you could see the shine of the Nigger's skin as he moved to catch it.

"Follow me," said Dorval.

His tone made it an order. He went to the window and his tenants gathered around him. One of Madame Marchessault's breasts was squashed against his shoulder. Barnabé kicked his children to get them closer to Dorval; Dupont-la-France said, "All the same, night-time in Montreal simply isn't like night-time in Paris"; the Laterreur Brothers had an arm around each other's waist, very polite; Cowboy was quietly singing an obscene song into La Vieille's ear.

"Before you," said Dorval, "you have the skyscrapers. That's where capitalism lives. Listen."

Dupont-la-France shrugged his shoulders.

"Listen. Do you hear a voice?"

"No," they said, rather disturbed.

"You don't hear a voice? But you follow all its orders like a bunch of goddam slaves!"

They looked at one another, insulted.

"It's the voice of capitalism."

Doubt thickened the veil that alcohol had already drawn over their eyes.

He stretched out his arm and offered to the future the bottle he was holding, then brought it to his mouth. His gesture was copied unanimously. The beer gurgled down into gullets whose thirst would never be quenched.

"What language does it talk, the voice of capitalism?" asked Dorval.

"English."

"Baby American Jesus," Strangler suddenly remember-ed, his hand still holding Killer's, "we forgot all about our fight."

"We're all going with the Laterreur Brothers."

When everyone had jumped into the old Packard it fell to its knees like an overburdened donkey. Cowboy, sitting on somebody's knees, tickled his guitar:

> *Un canadien errant*
> Tried eating an Anglais
> But then it made him sick
> And he threw up all day.

Dorval came hopping along with his cast and his crutch, trying to catch up with the others and get a hold on the Packard. He finally got onto the running-board. Everyone but the Nigger was piled inside like beans in a can, while Dupont-la-France clung to the car, holding onto his beret, and several of the Marchessault children shouted insults at everybody. Dorval twirled his crutch, shouting as they passed the buildings:

67

"Maudits Anglais!"

The bottles of beer that hadn't been emptied flew from mouth to mouth. The Laterreur Brothers weren't drinking. Suddenly pale, they were trying to revive the fire of violence within them in time for the fight.

"Baptême!" Dorval was amazed. "Even the beer we drink is English!"

But he didn't spit it out.

* * *

The Laterreur Brothers, blinded by the spotlights directed at the ring, couldn't see the assembled crowd, but they heard it breathing and moving and shouting all around them. Dorval's tenants shouted and waved to encourage them.

"Don't be afraid! We're with you!"

Killer and Strangler could make out the shrill voice of Dupont-la-France in the brouhaha.

"If they try to hurt ya bite the bastards!" This in the harsh little voice of La Vieille.

The Laterreur Brothers held back their smiles to maintain their mean appearance. They weren't alone now in the center of the rumbling swarming crowd. The MC grabbed the microphone.

"On my left, the honour of Québec, the ancestral genius of French-Canadian strength, weighing in at 597 pounds of solid muscle: the Laterreur Brothers!"

Applause.

"On my right, from Canada, weighing 609, the undisputed Canadian champions from one Atlantic to the other: the Gorgeous Glasscos."

A hail of insults, boos and threats reverberated through the arena to the ring.

The fate of the Québécois race was in the hands of the

Laterreur Brothers. In their biceps three hundred years of history trembled. And in their heads, Dorval's theory resounded with the rhythm of a crazy clock:

"Résistance! Résistance!"

At the referee's signal the Laterreur Brothers leaped as one onto the Gorgeous Glasscos. Blind and furious tanks. The Canadian combatants received them in their arms, carried them like babies to the ropes and let them drop to the floor of the arena: two bags of garbage. They no longer heard the voice of history. The fate of the Québécois race was lying in blood-red jerseys, fat hairy legs spread apart.

It was not until later that the Laterreur Brothers found the strength to open their eyes. They had been taken away in the Packard. Marchessault was at the wheel, Hildegarde was sitting on Killer's lap caressing Strangler's chest, and Dorval was standing on the running-board surrounded by humiliated children and shouting blasphemies.

"Mes Christ! Mes ciboires! Mes baptêmes! Mes Vierge! Mes Jésus! You won a battle but we're going to win the war!"

The air slapped at his face and whistled past his ears; Dorval felt strong. If he had wanted, he could have pushed back the wall of buildings that hid the sky from him. The Laterreurs' defeat brought back the memory of a slap on his face, and his heart was far away, being trampled somewhere in an unknown room by that whore Mignonne Fleury.

"Résistance!"

* * *

The Packard, parked in front of Dorval's house, emptied silently. The humiliated tenants were eager to get back to their flats. In the oppressive silence, feeble lights appeared in some of the windows.

"Look," said Dorval. "The city's standing up in its own shit. See the English capitalists' skyscrapers? They're coming down on us. We're gonna be buried. All us little guys are gonna be wiped out."

"We got to resist," said La Vieille. "Nobody's gonna bury me till I'm nailed inside my coffin."

Killer Laterreur was holding Strangler's aching head. "In our contract with the Gorgeous Glasscos it was written out specifically that we were supposed to win the fight."

"The Gorgeous Glasscos are *Anglais* and *Anglais* don't respect contracts," said Hildegarde.

"Go on and argue if you want," said Barnabé, "me, I'm going to study. Construction starts soon and when I finish my correspondence course I'll be a qualified man with a trade and a job and a salary. I'll be a *man*."

"At last!" Hildegarde sighed. "I'll be sleeping with a man that's got a job and a diploma."

"Dupont!" Dorval ordered. "Pass out the beer."

He was applauded as loudly as the Laterreur Brothers before their fight.

"Tonight," he went on, "we were all humiliated along with the Laterreurs."

They nodded their heads in agreement, not yet daring to use words to record the true facts.

"But that insult is nothing compared with what's waiting for us. When the skyscrapers come down this far . . . ."

Convinced that the moment was serious they pressed around Dorval, drinking in his words as avidly as his beer. He explained his new tactic: better attack than be attacked. So, attack. But who? He did not immediately name the enemy.

"Who? Spit out his name! Who?"

The chorus of tenants exclaimed:

"Les Anglais!"

The Nigger's door slammed. Dorval served more beer.

70

Then he gave the signal for the attack:

"The hunt is on. You know how the government gives a bounty to wolf-hunters: they buy ears by the pair. Well, I personally will give a special bounty to any of you that brings me back a pair of *Anglais* ears and I'll give the women an extra little premium in kind!"

Hildegarde Marchessault chortled; Barnabé objected.

"My future is in studying."

"The future," Dorval interjected, "is being decided today."

Barnabé tore himself away from his book, Cowboy picked up his guitar and the Laterreur Brothers were already far away.

"Don't forget: one ear doesn't count. I want the whole pair."

They scattered in the night, sniffing out the paths that would lead them past some *Anglais*. They hurried towards the City, along streets and lanes where it would be easy to spot an *Anglais* among the mixture of cars and pedestrians, pull him into a dark corner and twist his ears, saying: "If I hurt you it's because your great-great-great-great-grandfather stole my country and I'm going to get it back one of these days."

It was so dark in their lane: Strangler Laterreur squeezed Killer's hand affectionately to give him courage. A pale light seeped out of some heavily curtained windows. The Laterreur Brothers walked more slowly. Each door, darker than the night, was like a gulf plastered with threatening shadows. Someone was walking behind them. They heard no sound, not even breathing, only a silence that pressed against their backs as heavily as a stare. Killer squeezed Strangler's hand. The ring had taught them the power of a ruse: they turned around abruptly, their big bears' paws ready to strike. A man was following them.

"Do you speak English?" Killer roared.

"Yes."

The man had whispered, his throat knotted with fear. The Laterreur Brothers came crashing down on him as they had not succeeded with the Canadian wrestlers in the ring. They crushed the little man to the ground under the weight of their triumphant bellies.

"It's easy," said Killer.

"We nabbed our *Anglais* already," said Strangler.

A muffled voice that seemed to come from below the pavement was squealing:

"Hang goong apoon floon na ni noon!"

"Mama!" Strangler exclaimed. "It's an *Anglais* from China!"

The street was suddenly alight. The Laterreur Brothers stood up.

"The police!"

They cleared out, pursued by a police car, its rotating red light whipping at the black wall. The little man hopped along behind them, waving a threatening fist.

"Hai anakoong alaloon shan tikoo han ban ting doon dong ding!"

In another lane La Vieille, ambushed in a recess in a wall, was waiting for her *Anglais*. It was one of those lanes where the kids won't tolerate a single unbroken street-light. La Vieille was worried.

"No *Anglais* ain't coming to a dark corner like this. It's a hole for French Canadians."

Standing close to the wall, La Vieille became shadow and silence. Far away in the night the city was snoring. La Vieille was on the look-out: her heart was beating as it had when she was a young girl and she could hear her fiancé's footsteps on the balcony. Somebody all in black was coming through the night. His heels tapped feverishly against the road. He was already facing La Vielle, who stuck her head out of the shadow."

"Hey," she called out in French, "can you talk English?"

"Yes."

La Vieille took an excessively youthful leap and threw herself onto the passerby. Stammering a lament that was incomprehensible but almost caressing, the passerby in an attempt to defend himself, lifted La Vieille's skirt, causing her to be raised up into the air and brought back vigorously to earth again. Suddenly she felt such a potent strength penetrating between her thighs that she spread her arms, proclaiming, *"Vive l'Angleterre!"* The passerby put her down on the road, moved around on top of her, groaned, shouted: *"Confiteor Deo omnipotenti."*

Suddenly, as though lacerated by a heavy whip, he exclaimed: *"Deus, miserere nobis!"*

La Vieille opened her eyes but she could not see the face that was breathing above her own; she thought that if all the *Anglais* were like this one she could spend the whole night hunting them.

"Are you a real *Anglais*?" she asked.

The passerby pressed her breast and went away intoning, *"Kyrie eleison!"*

La Vieille wanted to call back her prey but she didn't speak English. She returned to her hiding-place.

"That was a real *Anglais*. He just talked English. He had nice English manners too. Gentle."

The passerby, a winged angel in his nocturnal joy, had flown away. La Vieille couldn't see him stop under a streetlight to check the long row of buttons on his seminarian's soutane.

Dorval was limping along a street that he knew very well, towards a whorehouse he had never visited before. He went in and drank a beer.

"Jos, I got an urge to screw England. Have you got an *Anglaise*, a real one, built like a plum pudding?"

The barman made a telephone call in English.

"Number 28's expecting you."

Dorval picked up his crutch, climbed up the stairs and knocked on the door of number 28.

"Come in, my love."

He pushed the door open. Throwing out his chest, slinging his crutch over his shoulder and stiffening his legs, he said,

"Good night, madam."

This *Anglaise* wouldn't escape his net. Of course he wouldn't bring a pair of ears back from his escapade but he would be able to tell how he'd sunk the Québécois tool that was starting to shine in his trousers into the body of an *Anglaise*; he would describe in loving detail how the beautiful *Anglaise* had writhed on the mattress, how she had been paralyzed by his caresses, how she had wept under the delicious torture, pleading in the agony of her pleasure but begging Dorval not to put an end to the punishment, imploring him to plunge deeper, more furiously, shouting that he took her breath away and begging him to put out the fire that was consuming her. Ah! how Dorval would tell the story of his hunt!

"Children, I'm going to tell you the story of a chase that's far from chaste, ha, ha!"

Ah! this *maudite Anglaise* was going to learn something about Québécois domination.

"Get undressed," said the voice.

Dorval couldn't see anyone but he could hear garters snapping behind a screen. He moved forward.

"You give me twenty bucks first. If you want me all naked it's twenty-five."

"*Baptême,* even in a whorehouse we get screwed by the *Anglais*!"

At the same time his proud, well-tempered sword of honour was tearing a hole through his trousers. He reflected that it was always easier for French Canadians to give than to ask.

"If you want me completely naked, it's free," said Dorval.

"I don't like beggars in my bed."

Dorval threw twenty-five dollars onto the bed. The girl left her screen without looking at her customer. She picked up the bills, unfolded them, smoothed them out and put them into a bag that she then replaced under the mattress. Then she dropped onto the bed. Dorval shot forward like someone about to pillage Ali Baba's cave.

"Dorval!"

"Mignonne Fleury!"

She was standing on the bed, waving the bedside lamp. Her nostrils were flaring like an angry dragon's. Dorval hid his sex with one hand; with the other he searched for his crutch, unable to stand on just one leg.

"But I asked for an *Anglaise*."

"Whoremonger! Rapist! Help!"

He moved the hand that was hiding his sex and, using his crutch, he walked towards Mignonne.

"Since you pass yourself off as an *Anglaise* I'll give you the little treatment I was saving for her."

He dropped the crutch and hurled himself at Mignonne, using his good foot.

"Goddammit woman—I love you."

The bedside lamp came crashing down on his head and the bulb smashed into electric crumbs that crackled around him in the total darkness. Dorval had grabbed a leg. His hand recognized the beginning of the calf.

"Mignonne Fleury, you're as cold as steel, but goddam you I'm going to turn you into red-hot iron!"

"Help!"

Dorval realized that he was holding not one of Mignonne Fleury's legs but a bed-post. He groped around in the dark, found his crutch and ran to the window. He could no longer see Mignonne Fleury who had disappeared into the night as though it were the folds of a curtain.

"Mignonne Fleury, I love you! I love you, Mignonne Fleury!"

The night replied with a woman's laughter. He heard her footsteps tumbling down the fire-escape. Leaning on his crutch and furiously clenching his toes in their cast he ran down the stairs as though he were plunging into the void.

"Rape!"

Mignonne's steps resounded on the iron stairs, lower down.

"I love you!"

Suddenly, he was stunned as though something hard had hit him: it was the beam of a searchlight. He remembered that he was naked, wearing nothing but the cast on his foot.

"I'm bare naked. Turn that off, goddammit!"

"Get down outta there or we'll bring you down by the balls!"

"Christ! When the whores don't want it the cops come running. What manners, *Monsieur le Curé*!"

"No insults! We're the law."

At the end of the same lane Hildegarde and Barnabé Marchessault heard screaming tires and sirens, but the police car didn't disturb their *Anglais*-hunt. They advanced slowly, he skinny, she waddling in her fat, both holding their breath, taking a hundred precautions as though the night had leaves and branches. Ahead of them there were voices speaking English. A man and a woman were holding each other so close that they made one round shadow in the night. The man said something and the woman burst out in a laugh that was not French-Canadian. Then their round shadow divided; the woman escaped, laughing, and the man, who was also laughing, went off on the other side of the street.

"My heart's dancing a jig: listen!" said Hildegarde.

"Shut your trap if you want me to hear anything!"

Hildegarde took Barnabé's hand and pressed it against her heart, into the soft flesh of her enormous teat. He whispered, "Tease!"

"Impotent!"

Barnabé removed his hand.

"I'm attacking," said Hildegarde.

"Wait for your order," said Barnabé in a voice like a general's. "We'll divide the catch: I take the woman, you take the man."

In the back pocket of his pants Barnabé was carrying, as he always did, the hammer he had been given along with a screwdriver as free accessories for his correspondence course. He held out the hammer to his wife.

"Take this. The *Anglais* have hard heads. Don't hit too hard or you'll bust the hammer."

They divided their forces. Hildegarde made her way among the heaped-up garbage cans and accumulated piles of rubbish. Barnabé wove through the cars in the parking-lot. A lighted window here and there prevented the darkness from being total. Wings were quivering in Hildegarde's back. This game of hunting *Anglais* was so much fun—as much fun as . . . Hildegarde didn't want to think about that when she was hunting. What a man, that Dorval, who had invented the *Anglais*-hunt! Hit an *Anglais*! Her pleasure reeked of sacrilege.

Barnabé picked up a stray brick. Obviously he wouldn't bring the ears of the *Anglaise* back to Dorval. Dorval always went too far. He'd just bring him a trophy from the hunt: her underpants or her brassiere.

Sitting astride the fence Barnabé scrutinized the night with its spots of light. The *Anglaise* was coming. He jumped off the fence, ran to hide under a staircase and waited, stuck against the wall.

Hildegarde walked close to the wall, trying to make herself invisible in the night. She could distinguish the dark shape of the *Anglais* just a few steps away from her.

Barnabé was clinging to the wall, invisible. He was so close to the *Anglaise*. His hair was standing on end.

"Do you speak English?" he asked, grasping his brick firmly.

The *Anglaise* raised her arm very high and Barnabé was struck by a hammer. He fell down at Hildegarde's feet. She got to her knees to contemplate her prey. Just as she recognized Barnabé a weakened hand, armed with a brick, split open her forehead.

The *Anglais* couple, walking along the street, found Hildegarde and Barnabé Marchessault moaning, their faces all bloody.

"Help! Help!" cried the *Anglaise,* in tears.

Three streets away there was a neon sign with just a few letters illuminated; only connoisseurs knew that they designated the Taverne Alberta. Dupont-la-France had always expressed profound disgust for these smoky rooms where the drinkers always made the same grunting noises whether they were talking, laughing or belching. English sounds brushed past his ears. His search for game had led him to the Taverne Alberta: he stood in the doorway listening, then went in, analyzed the battle sites and went to a corner where the people were speaking English.

"Bring me a glass of draft," he ordered, "well chilled and not too strong. And no head, please."

"Son of a bitch, it's a Frenchman. Boys! We got a fuckin frog here," announced Giguère the proprietor.

"It's my turn," said the waiter, bringing Dupont two drafts.

"Guys, let's drink to the honour of France!"

Dupont raised his glass, drank a mouthful with a grimace and put the glass back on the table, but the others were still drinking. To conform with the folkways of the country, Dupont swallowed another mouthful. The others were still drinking. Finally he managed to drain his glass like everyone else.

"Please stand drinks all around," said a big man who seemed to be talking in his sleep.

Several glasses were raised in Dupont's honour, and so as not to look effeminate he drained his in one gulp.

"Hey you, big guy, if you're with RCA Victor you can buy a round; I'm with the CNR so I can buy one too." He switched to English. "I am able to pay as much beer as you can. Okay? Understand?"

Glasses piled up on Dupont-la-France's table and he felt obliged to drink them in order not to be discourteous. He was even polite.

"I've travelled all over Europe and I've never tasted such good beer. It's the champagne of beers."

"You're too fucking polite; you can't be a real Frenchman."

"I've been French as far back as our ancestors the Gauls who drank beer like pigs."

Dupont was dizzy. He felt as though he were looking at his companions from the top of the Eiffel Tower.

"I went to France," said one of the drinkers in English. All his teeth were gold and he was missing an arm. "I know France very well: I went with the Army. To the Queen, salute!"

Beer glasses were raised high in the air. Only a few separatist arms remained on the table. Dupont, because he was an immigrant, had to outdo the others. He presented two arms and two glasses to the Queen.

"What the hell are you doing here in Canada?" asked Giguère the proprietor.

Dupont was as full of beer as a barrel. Opening his mouth to reply he had the impression that the beer was running out.

"I came to hunt. Bang bang. You know?"

"You're hunting? You won't find no partridges in here; me, I hunt partridges every year, down in the Beauce. That's a sport for a man. But I never caught nothing yet."

Dupont drank again.

"Come on, what are you hunting for?" In English.

"*Anglais.* English. I am hunting *Anglais,* you understand? I collect their ears. English ears, you know?"

"You goddam Frenchman, get out of here. And don't ever stick your nose in my tavern again," said Giguère.

"Get out of here!" In English.

"*Maudit Français,* don't go stirring up trouble here in our free country."

Several hands seized Dupont-la-France and threw him outside. The shock of his landing on the sidewalk burst the barrel of beer and he urinated in his torn trousers. Dupont was still; he was sleeping like a child in the gentle warmth of his bed in France.

Meanwhile, Cowboy was sitting on the doorstep of the Toronto-Dominion Bank, grumbling at Dorval's childish game. From time to time, to punctuate the sentiments he was expressing, he would pluck a string on his guitar.

"The *Anglais* never stopped me from singing (do mi sol do). It's true what Dorval says, though; they own the skyscrapers (do). It's true their skyscrapers come all the way down the hill and they're gonna crush us (la si re). But at least they're air-conditioned (do si fa si fa). It's better than the stink of dead rats in the wall (do). The *Anglais* never stopped a French Canadian from singing what he wanted (do). Because they don't understand a goddam word!"

> I sing to kill time
> That I got on my hands
> And when I see an *Anglais*
> I sing: go to hell
> *Maudit Anglais.*

Cowboy was abstaining from the Anglais-hunt and his decision was irrevocable. He got up and slung his guitar over his shoulder. The sound-box struck against the glass door. The strings quivered. Had he broken the guitar? He examined it. Nothing. It hadn't been hurt and the glass door was intact, but the burglar alarm had gone off.

That was why some policemen took him to Station 10-12, to the common bird-cage where he found Dorval and all his tenants, even La Vieille who, after she had been raped by a seminarian she thought was English because he spoke Latin, had gone to give thanks to God for her great joy. But she had been unable to leave the Church without taking as a souvenir the lily from the feet of the Virgin.

Everyone knew Mignonne Fleury. The policemen greeted her with respect and she was the first to be invited to leave the common cell. Dorval watched her parade down a corridor where greetings came pouring out the open door-ways. Her bottom, quivering under her tight dress, shimmered like sunlight in this cellar where the City stowed away its rejects. Dorval began a harangue.

"There's no justice in this goddam capitalist country. I'm telling you a woman's behind is stronger than the truth. That's what makes the law. That's what determines the course of justice."

"Shut your trap. We're trying to sleep."

"We don't give a shit about you and your behinds!"

In the morning the cage door was opened but the hunters of *Anglais* ears did not leave. They were detained, interrogated, not given any food. They had been caught in the act of terrorism, but no one had found any weapons or subversive literature or explosives on them.

"We were just having some fun," Dorval pleaded.

"The Revolution," said one of the inspectors who was sucking on a candy for his digestive problems, "is not a game."

"We just wanted a laugh, *Monsieur la police.*"

"You wanted to cut off ears for a laugh?"

"Yes, *Monsieur la police.* Me, I say a free country is a country where you can laugh."

"Cutting ears off poor harmless *Anglais* that already have enough trouble trying to understand our language—you call that funny?"

"The *Anglais* capitalists take our houses and our land. Taking their ears, it's the least we can do, *Monsieur la police.*"

"And what about order and harmony and national unity?"

"If order means that little kids have to get down on their hands and knees and kiss capitalist asses, me, I say, let's have disorder! *Vive la Révolution!*"

"Don't try to intimidate the Enquirer, you big son of a bitch. You're in a free country big guy, but you're still in jail. Terrorist, ear-stealer, raper of innocent girls, insulter of the law!"

"Don't try to intimidate the prisoner, *Monsieur la police.*"

During these difficult moments of human incomprehension Dorval told himself that wars could indeed break out between different peoples if brothers who spoke the same language couldn't manage to understand one another. One thing gave him some comfort, though: the thought of the little garden he and his tenants had ploughed and planted together. Sometimes he felt so attached to his garden that he wanted to stay in jail for days so that when he came out he could watch the green plants bursting out of the newly alive earth.

The enquiry lasted for three days; then the patriotic ear-hunters were set free. They piled triumphantly into a taxi and when they were near their house they noticed a fleet of bulldozers levelling their garden.

* * *

Steam-shovels and trucks came to join the bulldozers. The orders were given by little sun-tanned men who appeared to be drunk; Dorval spent hours hurling invective at them but all they could hear was mechanical groans. Then mechanical cranes with rotating baskets arrived; their huge teeth began to dig a trench. Fat pipes filled the trench to overflowing with brown mud that was soon replaced by cement poured from the cement-mixers into the trenches. Other cranes, even higher, arrived, with their gigantic hammers; with repeated blows they sank steel stems into the deepest layer of clay, then into the bedrock. The machines were relentless, eternal: the crane raised its hammer, let it drop with the sound of smashed metal because of the clay that was caught between its teeth; the motors were furious and the hammer struck. It lasted for days and days. The bulldozers piled up earth, cranes came and filled the trucks with it and the trucks trampled the ground and carried the dirt away. It never stopped. Day and night, steel struck against rock, day and night the motors whined like exhausted beasts and day and night it was a furious flock that dug at the earth.

83

To Dorval and his tenants it seemed that the digging was going on right under their house. Cracks ran up to the ceiling, in the plaster; the walls themselves were torn and the house was floating on a sea of noise. In the refrigerator the bottles of beer danced on the shelves and struck against each other with clinking sounds.

"When I went across the sea to fight the war there wasn't as much ground-swell as this. Ah! baby Jesus! I'd rather not remember that. I did everything to paint over all my memories so they wouldn't be memories any more. I wanted a clean start, with a memory that was naked like a bald man's head or a baby's bum. Awake, asleep, I always stayed drunk. *Vierge!* how I drank. If the trip had lasted any longer there would have been more beer inside me than there was water around the boat. And I wasn't the only one. There were hundreds of boys like me, just as drunk; there were thousands of young guys on that boat, all squeezed in like sausages in a box. Was I at the front of the boat or the back? On the port or the starboard side: I never found out. But I was at the bottom: when I put my hand down on the floor I could feel the sea the way you know what a person feels like through his clothes. We were at the very bottom: we were stacked up in our pallets with our noses in our neighbour's ass. Children, I felt like a stranger as far away from home as he could be, even though I was with guys from my own country that were wearing the same boots, the same shit-coloured khaki pants and we were all going to fight the same war: not a goddam one of them spoke the same French language I do. The only time we all made the same sounds was when we vomited and our guts came out our noses. And we were forbidden to go up on deck and unwind in the fresh air. We were closed in like eggs, like we were in our mother's bellies, a mother that kept rolling downstairs for twenty days. And they all talked English, just like the good Lord talks Latin. Like everybody else I learned seven words of English: john, yes my captain, king, gun, shit. But I wasn't as comfortable as I was in a haystack with my girl! I had to forget where I came from. From time to time some words would fly from one pallet to another, floating from one end of the boat to the other like a bird. If a mouth-organ was playing somewhere the black bird swallowed up the song and everybody laid down on his bunk again. The black bird was when one of the boats in our fleet got sunk. The sadness spread over our faces like butter on toast. Once the boat next to ours was burnt up like a match. The people in our boat that knew the ways of the sea could feel the undercurrents. Everybody threw himself into his bed like it was his mother's arms. We were so scared we were shivering from nose-hole to asshole. Then me, I got up. It wasn't that I was less scared than anybody else. (They say, *mes enfants,* that being scared is a sign of courage.) Anyway, I starting reciting a few litanies you'll never hear in Church.

" *'Tabernacle plein de marde de Jésus! Ciboire de crosse de pape!'*

"And then from the other end of the boat I heard,

" *'Baptême d'enfant de chienne!'* At last, somebody else that talked French!

"A guy came zigzagging through the pallets, because he was drunk and he was rolling. He came running up to me, out of breath:

" 'You talk French too, eh?'

"He was so close to me his mouth was practically stuck to my ear.

" 'I got something to tell you. Something I absolutely gotta say in French: the Germans are on the prowl. They're right underneath us now. We're gonna get blown up. We won't even get a chance to see the goddam war!'

"He was so sure that I began to believe him, but I didn't

85

want him to see it, so I said:

" 'We're gonna be heroes just like the generals. Them, they don't have to go to the war!'

"The bugger didn't even laugh.

" 'I come from Montmagny,' he says.

" 'Me, I come outta my mother!'

" 'I got blisters on my gums from talking English.'

"He offered me his flask and I drank a drop. He kept on talking:

" 'I'm scared of water like the devil's scared of holy oil. I don't wanta drownd to death in the water. I don't wanna fall in the ocean when the Germans come and blow us up. When the time comes I want you to shoot a bullet at me. There's gonna be a lot of panic. Explosions everywhere. I want you to kill me if the Germans don't do it first.'

"(*Mes enfants,* you know me pretty well; if I tell you that I, Dorval, pissed my pants right then, you'll understand me, right?) I answered,

" 'I couldn't do that. Even if you were an *Anglais.'*

" 'It's because you, you ain't scared of the water.'

"I looked at him. He understood me. He looked at me. I understood him. We swore an oath to each together by wringing each other's necks as we sang 'O Canada'.

"There was a hell of a swell. When I wasn't cursing the good Lord I was praying to him. I told myself, If we got out of the boat we'll get to the war and then we can stop being scared. Goddammit but there was a powerful swell. I asked the guy,

" 'How come you enrolled in His Majesty's Army?'

" 'To get the hell out of Montmagny. How about you?'

" 'To get the hell out of my mother's place. But right now with all the uproar down there I'd like to get the hell out of right here.'

" 'If the Germans blow us up the guys overseas won't

86

get their supply of cannon-fodder.'

"Me, I re-assured him,

" '*Hostie de tabernacle!* Every day I pray to the good Lord, from the bottom of my heart. We're absolutely gonna get to Europe.'

"His eyes were overflowing, his cheeks were wet and he was grimacing.

"What was his name? Do you know? Me, I never found out. While he was yelling his lungs out they announced that we were in Europe. He disappeared."

Dorval wiped away a tear that had come to him, no doubt impelled by the invading power of the past.

* * *

Now the hole was big enough to bury a whole village, its houses, its church, its inhabitants. There was a constant, penetrating wave of noise surrounding it; Dorval's tenants seemed like slightly mad deaf-mutes in a deserted place of refuge. Without speaking they made broad, uncoordinated gestures in the uproar. They spoke only to themselves. Not even the shouting and whining of the Marchessault children could be heard.

"You, La Vieille, you're already deaf; the noise can't bother you any."

"When they nail me in my coffin I'll put up with not hearing, not before."

Barnabé Marchessault was impatient to finish his course. The machines were calling to him from the bottom of the hole. Despite the mechanical throbbing he read brochures day and night, he studied drawings, scrutinized diagrams and plans, took apart his motor and reassembled it in an oily fever: the pieces were spread out on the floor, on the table, among the plates and milk-bottles; he was so absorbed by his work and the uproar of the machines that he didn't hear his bed-springs creaking beneath the amorous tremblings of Hildegarde and Dupont-la-France. No one scolded Barnabé now for hammering the recalcitrant bolts of his motor; there was always a power-hammer in the hole that was making more noise than he was.

Dynamite explosions shook the house. Over the front door, enthroned in her niche, there was statue of the Blessed Virgin.

"Sure I'm an atheist inside and out, but I'm no goddam bigot."

One evening the good Blessed Virgin of plaster, no doubt stunned by the surrounding tremors, lost her balance, swayed and fell onto Dorval's crippled foot. Bits of plaster went flying in all directions and La Vieille could not separate what belonged to Dorval from what belonged to the Virgin.

Finally, the framework of the house, shaken on all sides, was totally awry. The windows were broken. When the wind blew it blew right through the house, grey with dust. In the morning everyone had dry throats, and their saliva tasted of sand. Dust had insinuated into cupboards and drawers. The Nigger didn't dare leave his room. Dorval had seen him at his window, dusting his body with a white cloth. Dorval could feel the grit in all his joints.

One day Cowboy appeared, guitar over his shoulder, suitcase in hand.

"*Salut!* I can't sing here no more. *Salut,* Dorval."

"Go on," said Dorval. "Go see if you can sing in peace somewhere else."

"It's a big world."

"Yeah, I've seen the world. Sure it's big. But it's full of people that keep telling you to shut your trap."

Cowboy pinched the strings of his guitar and sang something, but a furious motor began to cough with angry rasping sounds. Dorval could hear nothing more. He shouted:

"Go to the Devil! And if you run into Mignonne Fleury when you get there, tell her she can stay too!"

She had not returned since the night of the Anglais ear-hunt.

"You can all go. Get down off your crosses and just fuck off. But me, I'm staying, even if the goddam capitalists throw my house into their hole. But I'm staying on my own two feet. I'll be standing in mud right up to my teeth, but I'll be on my own two feet! I'll resist!"

"Me, I'll go on resisting till they nail me inside my coffin."

The Laterreur Brothers spent more and more time away from home. Several days later they came back from the Gaspé, from Abitibi and the Beauce covered with bruises and bloody bandages, black-eyed but smiling and talking to one another with great affection. They had never fought so many fights: fights every day, twice on Saturday and Sunday; they drove to the four corners of Québec. If they let themselves be trounced from one frontier to the other and come home with more bruises on their bodies than there are lakes on the map of Québec instead of shutting themselves inside their room, putting their hair in rollers and parading around in lace panties and brassieres, Dorval supposed they must have some good reason for it: the Laterreur Brothers had a passionate appetite for money. One night he surprised Killer and Strangler entwined against one another and staring blankly at the pit that had been hollowed out by the machines. Dorval thought they looked like young virgins contemplating a wedding-dress. They were dreaming of the future before this hole and their dream struck Dorval like a bolt of lightning:

"Goddam you, you're already deciding what floor your little love-nest will be on. One day I'll hang both your two big moose-heads on my living-room wall. While everybody else is fighting you two ball-less wonders are singing lovesongs to the capitalists' skyscraper. You come and dream about a little bedroom in the skyscraper on the two-thousandth floor, a little bedroom as pink as your panties. While we're carrying on the Resistance you pick up your nickels and quarters to buy yourselves the right to climb up to the two-thousandth floor and piss on us. Goddam you! Even if the people get down on their knees I'm standing on my own two feet, like a man. Listen carefully to what I'm shouting in the face of the world: a man that can stand on his own two feet and get a hard-on is bigger than any skyscraper."

Why was Mignonne Fleury not there to hear Dorval's words crackling in the night like flags? What bed was she in, with sheets where she welcomed one man after another, listening to the stories of their lives with the bored ear of a confessor who has heard everything, already ready to forgive, with the tired gestures of someone who is tired of blessing. She must think of Dorval sometimes: he thought about her so often. He went up to his room to breathe in the odour of her absence. He put his hand on the bed with its wool and cretonne cover, caressing the sinuous idea of Mignonne's body. Or he would pick up a long reddish hair that had fallen onto the linoleum and twist it around his neck. Sometimes he would open a drawer and contemplate Mignonne's underwear; it seemed to be alive and breathing like flesh. He came downstairs again drunk, repeating the name of Mignonne Fleury.

"To hell with you, you two little girls with beards; you stare at that hole with eyes like a cow sizing up a bull. Resist, *bon Dieu de Christ!* Every shovelful of dirt they took out of that hole is thrown at us to bury us."

"Who's doing all that yelling?" Strangler asked.

"I can't hear, there's too much noise," Killer shouted in reply.

There was also the rough little autumn wind sharpening itself on the ground that was already turning hard. The bulldozers and trucks at the bottom of the hole looked like big overloaded insects climbing painfully up or down the spiral path that went around its walls.

"To hell with that hole," said Dorval. "They shoulda stopped the construction and thrown all the big guys in there, into a pile of living shit. But the whole earth isn't big enough to bury all those sons of bitches."

Dorval came as close as he could to the edge of the pit; his toes touched the rim and his belly drifted over it like a balloon. He opened his fly and, proclaiming, *"Résistance,"* he pissed. The Laterreur Brothers observed him, looked at each other: with a single gesture they urinated into the hole with a conviction no less generous than Dorval's.

"Résistance! Résistance!"

Dorval was sad:

"We should have pissed a whole Niagara."

He put his arms on the shoulders of the two wrestlers and pressed them to his chest like a loving mother. He invited them to drink a beer.

"When we went over to Europe there was a swell like all the saints in Heaven but I could never remember if there was a swell when we came home. There musta been. But the thought of La Pucelle must have affected me more than the swell. That whore La Pucelle! I thought at least she could have said goodbye to a brave soldier that came from Canada to save her country, asking with tears in her eyes, 'Give me something to remember you by.' She could've even asked me for my picture, but no! She was as dry as a school-teacher: 'Do you think you're going to speed up the class struggle by trying to fiddle with my breasts? Don't think you're a man just because your little dinkus can stand up. It's the whole man who must rise! It's the entire

91

people that must get to its feet! All the nations on earth!"

"So I hid my fly behind my hands and kept telling myself that a factory belongs to its workers, not to the Boss. La Pucelle taught me that and I'd read it on my toilet-paper too. La Pucelle had the soul of a school-teacher, but her body, her body!

"When the war was over they were going to throw the left-over cannon-fodder into the garbage-cans. After we'd saved Europe for them. 'Who is France?' La Pucelle asked. 'The proletarians with grease on their hands or the people that wear white gloves? Who did we win the war for? Who will take the spoils?'

"Did I get any of the spoils? And how about the French Canadians that stayed behind in Normandy? Did they get their share? Who shared the victory: the dirty hands or the ones in white gloves? How many guys with dirty hands were dead? How many *messieurs* with white gloves?

"The war isn't over! That's what Jeanne-la-Pucelle told me. I can still hear her voice and I'm telling you: there's no goddam swell that's going to bother me. They can dig my grave right under my feet and I'll still say *Résistance!*"

* * *

A few days later Dorval received a card postmarked Sainte-Emelie-de-l'Energie: "Dear lanlord, we're sorry we broke your hart we'll stay under your rufe as long as you. Last night we got beat real hard but we're consoling each other. love Killer and Strangler Laterreur."

The same day Barnabé Marchessault received a long-awaited letter. As he and Hildegarde could not believe what they read they came, weeping hot tears, looking for Dorval.

92

"Dear Sir,

We regret to announce that the learned official markers of our reputed institution have judged the answers submitted by you to our examination questionnaire to be unsatisfactory. We are very disappointed to find ourselves in the position of being unable supply you your certificate of competence. However, since the goal of our institution is educational, not lucrative, and since we are essentially and positively at the service of our student-clients and future graduates, we are pleased to inform you that your failure makes you eligible for our course No.XM1234 which we offer to you with the guarantee (98%) that you will pass your examination. So don't be one of those men without a future who let themselves be beaten by one setback. Be tenacious. Besides, our psycho-calligraphers, who have diplomas and accreditation in their own right, have informed us that the handwriting on your examination reveals all the signs of inevitable success because of the consistency that is characteristic of your intelligence. To enroll on the list of chosen students to whom we will open the road to future success, you need only send us the modest sum (an investment, really) of $500.00. We ask you, however, NOT to include the usual tax of 16.8%, which we hold on account. Thus as a former student of our school you will be given priority on your first lesson in course No.XM1234.

"And we wish you every success!"

Dorval gave the letter back to Hildegarde without finding the words they were waiting for. Barnabé went back up to his kitchen. She remained, leaning against Dorval. She came closer and collapsed against him. The soft mounds of her breasts gave off a comforting warmth and her belly was shaken by sobs. Perhaps it was because of Hildegarde's tears that flowed onto his neck that he didn't enclose her in his arms. He barely caressed her hair. Hildegarde's breathing, all

93

shaken by her tears, became choked. She took a step backwards:

"I think I'm dying."

She took Dorval's hand and pressed it against her breast.

"Can you feel? My heart's practically stopped beating. That bad news gave me an infracture. I'm dying!"

She took Dorval's other hand and put it on her other breast.

"Barnabé Marchessault is killing me; he's never been a man."

She pulled up her skirt. Dorval's house wanted to topple over into the excavation.

"He can't even get it up. He can't make that motor run any more than he can make me . . ."

She put Dorval's hand between her legs.

"He's condemned me to misery, me and the kids, to poverty . . ."

Dorval removed his hand from between Hildegarde's thighs:

"Barnabé isn't the one that's condemning you to poverty. He's a condemned man too."

She grabbed his hand and put it back between her legs.

"I'm telling you, from the beginning of time there's been people feeding on your misery."

Hildegarde wasn't crying now.

"Goddam male animals! When a woman needs a little affection Marchessault runs and gets his screwdriver and his wrench, Dupont-la-France says prayers to the Holy Apple and you, you make a political speech. Mignonne Fleury's the only woman I know that's happy!"

Trailing her heavy burden of spite Hildegarde went back to her apartment. Dorval watched her dress swelling over her buttocks with little shudders that drove him wild. He was softening.

94

"Hildegarde, don't go."

Why had he not heeded her when she was pressed against him? Why did he not let himself disappear in her like a swimmer in clear water?

"Hildegarde!" he begged.

"I'm going to console myself with a real man."

"Hildegarde!"

"But I'll take your picture before you go."

Bending over she raised her skirt and the white rounds of her buttocks glowed for a moment. His eyes dazzled, Dorval just had the strength to say in a choked voice:

"Go get yourself tickled by the devil! We aren't going to light up the Revolution by rubbing our bellies together!"

Hildegarde hesitated on the staircase. Would she come down again? He thought she would, but she disappeared on Dupont's landing. Dorval, in despair, went to get himself a beer.

"Ah, Mignonne Fleury, I want you! I want a real woman with an apron around her middle and curls and panties that don't come off at the slightest breeze and a good smell of beef cooking in a pot with cabbage and onions and garlic."

Sitting in his rocking-chair, forgetting the cold that had changed the puddles into brown ice, he drank a few more bottles of beer too. Every time he put his feet on the floor the entire universe swayed on its rockers too.

Upstairs, Barnabé Marchessault was standing in the middle of his kitchen, looking like a farmer mourning his best cow. He was contemplating his motor, all cleaned and polished, cleaner than the cloth on the table, perfectly put together, each piece rigorously put into its proper place with knowledge and love.

"I failed the examination. I'm a failure."

He searched in his trunk, emptied his tool-kit and spread

the tools in a semi-circle beside him, like a surgeon. With an implacable gesture he grabbed the air filter, walked to the window and hurled the object into the autumnal cold. He took hold of the fan-belt and got rid of it in the same way. He flung the propeller as deep into the hole as he could. He attacked the oil-drain, the valve-stem, the starter button, and as soon as a piece had been extirpated from the motor Barnabé hurled it into the hole. Next the injection pump, the dynamo, the drive-shaft, the spark plugs, the oil squeegee, the oil-housing were projected into the gulf by a devastating rage. Then the injector, the tripping device, the valve push-rod followed.

"Go to the devil!" Barnabé shouted.

Next went the accelerator, the cams; he was destroying his motor the way God will reduce the universe to bits at the end of the world, the way you chop up a chicken.

"To hell with this crankshaft!"

In the depths of the excavation the machines were working away with a thundering respiration.

Bolts whistled, pistons flew, the cylinder-head went sailing and valves leaped into the air. Because Barnabé couldn't set fire to this ungrateful pile of metal to which he had devoted a good part of his life, he had decided to bury it.

"Barnabé! What are you doing?"

It was Hildegarde.

"What am I doing?"

Barnabé flung her down onto the kitchen table. She couldn't resist so much strength so suddenly released. She gave in, drowning in pleasure.

"What a man!" she was amazed to murmur.

Barnabé didn't hear because of the uproar and the iron shrieks spilling out of the excavation.

* * *

One night the hole became silent. Snow was falling too and this time it would stay. No one was sleeping in Dorval's house: not the Marchessault children, who were yelling loud enough to tear the roof off, not La Vieille or Hildegarde or Barnabé. The Nigger paced around his room all night, as he had done all the time the work was being done, but this time you could hear the floor creaking under his feet. The great vault of the sky was silent; it seemed to conceal a silent threat, a cautious anger. The silence became painful. They turned over in their beds and then turned over again; they missed the racket as they would miss the air if it were taken away from them. They got up and wandered like the Nigger. The steps creaked under the weight of someone going downstairs. All the doors opened at once.

"It used to be quiet like this before a German bombardment."

"Hildegarde's wearing me out but she can't put me to sleep."

"All this peace is bothering me."

Dorval was not asleep. He was in his rocking-chair, drinking beer. He gestured to them to go to the refrigerator.

"I can hear the blood running through my veins," said Dupont.

"It sounds like piss," said Dorval.

There was so much silence around them, no one dared to laugh.

Hildegarde finally spoke. "Dorval's been insulting everybody for quite a while now. Insult the capitalists if you want, but not your own people."

Dorval, irritated, swallowed some beer. He rocked rather frantically, nervous and unhappy. His chair was a vehicle and he was using it to try to escape.

"Since these goddam machines shut up you can hear yourself think. They were digging their hole next door. I

97

watched them like somebody watching his own grave being dug. Sometimes I wanted to yell at them, 'Hey, that's too big for me! I'm big but I ain't no whale!' "

A dream passed before his eyes.

"It's so goddam quiet it's like the hole moved away somewhere else," said Hildegarde.

"It's moved inside," Dorval replied.

He began to rock furiously. Then, suddenly he leaped from his chair and ran out into the snow where the earth, still muddy, was losing its colour, like ink. He raised his fist towards the City that was blinking above him.

"Révolution!"

He went back inside, shaking his snow-covered feet.

"I'd be better off if I shut my mouth; the City's as deaf as a chamber-pot."

He served more beer and soon, everyone drunk, they went out into the snow and the huge silence of the night, clashing saucepans and bottles and shouting obscenities. Later, numbed by beer, they fell asleep remembering the loud noise of the machines.

* * *

When they woke up the immense tower of a crane was rising in the midst of the excavation. At the bottom men were trotting around. Tow-trucks came, loaded with steel shafts. Dump-trucks dumped hills of sand and gravel. Wooden beams were stacked up in yellow cubes and Dorval was aware of the scent of resin among the odours of muddy earth, gas leaks and burned oil. Here and there workers with red hands and white vapour coming out of their mouths were building transparent tents.

Mignonne Fleury had disappeared, Cowboy had gone to seek his fortune singing beneath the moon, the Laterreur

Brothers had fled. La Vieille would die soon, Dupont-la-France was waiting for the propitious moment when a naive spirit could slip away and plant orchards and apples, and the Marchessault family . . . Dorval could see only the youngest ones, their coarse grey diapers dragging in the snow; the others, whose legs were strong enough, had escaped towards the City and would come home only to sleep. The Marchessault family would leave too.

Dorval wanted to push his house into the hole. He fulminated:

"*Résistance! Révolution!* I'd like to stick them where you stick suppositories. Resist the capitalists—a goddam fine idea, but them, they got bulldozers and trucks and cranes and strong-boxes; they got more machines than I got ideas in my crazy head."

And cursing all the gods in Heaven, on earth, in the sea and in Hell he flung himself through his house, shouting,

"Out! I'm demolishing! Out!"

He opened La Vieille's door.

"Out! We're moving."

"I don't move till they nail me inside my coffin."

He pushed in Dupont-la-France's door.

"Dupont, fuck off. I'm demolishing."

Red and out of breath he arrived at the Marchessault flat.

"Pick up your corsets, fatso, then get your husband and kids together. Now. I'm demolishing. Setting fire to the place."

He threw a chair out the window.

"We're moving."

"Do we start by taking out the mattress?" Barnabé asked.

"Where are we going?" Hildegarde wanted to know.

"Go to the devil; me, I'm moving!"

There was a clothesline strung across the apartment, with diapers, shirts, sheets and underpants hanging to dry on it. Dorval broke the line, rolled the laundry into one big ball and threw it out the window.

"You too; you're moving just like the capitalists."

Hildegard wiped away a tear. Dorval bent his head.

"My heart's lower than my boots."

Hildegarde and Barnabé thought they could hear his roaring laugh but Dorval was sobbing and his words were broken by tears.

"I don't believe any more. Oh, I'm demolished, Hildegarde. Barnabé, I'm demolished.

Suitcase in hand, Dupont was savouring the taste of the insult he had prepared for Dorval. When he saw him weeping in Hildegarde's arms he swallowed his venom. Dupont put down his suitcase, took off his jacket and began to empty the Marchessault apartment: mattress, chairs, table, dishes, some chests of drawers, clothes. The men carried the heavy things, grimacing, groaning, sweating and swearing their way down the stairs. Hildegarde stood in the snow in front of the house giving orders.

"Put that here, put that there: over to the left, move it to the right; don't break nothing, impotents!" And the men, united in misfortune, obeyed a woman who was even unhappier than they were.

"We'll drink one last beer together," Dorval announced.

He came back with an armful of bottles. They drank in silence, sitting around the Marchessault's table that was standing in the snow. Only Dorval let a few words escape.

"I'm demolished."

Dupont shook hands with his friends and went away with his suitcases.

"Dorval!"

It was the raucous voice of La Vieille.

"Come and help me, Dorval."

She was wearing the flowered hat she kept for grand occasions. All her belongings were crammed into two paper shopping bags. Dorval bent down to pick them up.

"I'm going to the cemetery."

"You'll be better off there than you are here. It's quieter. It's cold in the winter, but it's cool in the summer too."

"Before I go, for the last time in my life I'd like to have a good taste of a man."

"What are you talking about, La Vieille? You'll go to Hell!"

"I'll go to Hell when they nail me in my coffin. Not before."

Trembling, La Vieille lay down on her bed from which all the covers had been removed.

"Dorval!" the old voice pleaded.

She lifted her skirt, opened her bony, wrinkled thighs. Dorval turned to the window, looking for help.

"Dupont-la-France! Dupont! We need you! Dupont!"

Dupont was already far away; he couldn't hear Dorval.

"It'll be the last time in my life, the last time before I die."

"I'll find you a good-looking lively young man your own age."

"You'll have to dig him up. Because there aren't many people my age still around. I really want to taste a man before the end. Dorval, just once."

With a dry gesture, Dorval opened his fly.

It seemed to him that this old woman's cold body reminded him of his youth. In a gentle flash it became warm.

La Vieille got up, replaced her flowered hat on her head, picked up her bags and went off singing, her coat open to the wind.

101

"Ah, there's still the goddam Nigger. We always forget that goddam Nigger."

He went downstairs. He hesitated before the Nigger's closed door; then, grumbling to himself, he pushed. The door struck against the wall of an empty room.

"*Baptême!* The Nigger's gone and I don't even know his name."

A shirt and a pair of trousers were folded over a chair. A jacket was hanging in the cupboard. His razor was on the chest of drawers, with some frizzy black hairs sticking out of it.

"Goddam Nigger!"

Dorval went back to his kitchen, drank some beer and wrote in big letters on the back of a calendar: DEMOLI-TION! Without even looking at the Marchessault family stomping around their furniture scattered in the snow, he nailed the poster to the front door and shut and bolted it from inside. Then he took refuge in the solitude of his kitchen. He had decided to get drunk. It would be his last night in his house and he already wanted to forget it.

"Mignonne Fleury, whose arms are you in now?"

Tomorrow he would set fire to his house. The capitalists wouldn't have the pleasure of getting their teeth into his house. The fire would leave nothing. The capitalists wouldn't make any money by selling the old wood and bricks. He wouldn't call the firemen. He would write to the insurance company: "Dear Sir, I wiped my ass with your insurance policies."

"It'll be like the war. A big fire, smoke, then nothing."

Later when he thought about it, he would wonder if it had really happened.

"Did I really go across the sea in a boat? Did I really fall out of the sky into France? Did Jeanne-la-Pucelle really exist? Mignonne Fleury—she exists, goddammit!"

This monologue whose branches kept growing longer and longer, more and more numerous, was not interrupted until he got up for another beer.

"They're gonna dig underneath, they're gonna build on top. I'll be buried like a dog turd."

Outside, under the black winter sky, the Marchessault family were sleeping rolled up in their blankets, muffled in sweaters and scarves and coats. The snow was blown by gusts of wind until it came close to the wool of the blankets. The light snowfall had gradually covered their beds. Dorval looked at the mounds formed by the Marchessaults and thought of a cemetery covered over by a snow-storm.

Remorse caught in his throat. His eyes filled with tears.

"Tomorrow they'll come back to my house. I'll give them their own apartment and Dupont's room and Cowboy's and La Vieille's too—she'll get herself picked up by some Sister. I'll even give them Mignonne Fleury's room."

In the morning Dorval, leaning back in his rocking-chair, was awakened by the violence of the light. Kicking aside the empty bottle he went to the window, yawning. The Marchessaults had gone.

* * *

Indifferent to its sap and to the seasons, the tree of the City, impelled by panic, continued to grow. Hundreds of hammers made a demented piano-music as they struck against nails in the boards of the framework that could finally be seen swaying at the end of cables, waiting to be put into place and adjusted. Other operations installed braces and stretched out girders or wove the framework on the beams; pebbles chirped in the cement-mixers and the buckets formed circles of mad birds before they were placed above the empty forms and poured concrete into the molds that were kept from opening and breaking apart beneath the enormous damp weight by joists, struts and props. Other workers, on their knees, stirred the cement. When it was dry other forms were assembled and props were put up; frameworks descended from the sky, underpinnings grew into a complex forest of iron and wood. Storey by storey the concrete tree grew, as indifferent as the sky to the prayers of a man in a small nearby house, pleading with a God in whom he did not believe.

"My God, if you think I'm an honest man, make that goddam pile of cement come falling down."

The concrete continued to grow.

"Even if you think I'm as big a rotten idiot as the capitalists, please God make it fall down."

The concrete was immutable, eternal, like God himself.

"My God, if you aren't deaf, make it stop growing."

But more storeys continued to be added.

"God, maybe you're the owner of that skyscraper. If that's the case I'm asking you to forgive a poor innocent man."

Dorval didn't feel the hand of a forgiving God on his brow.

"*Christ de bon Dieu,* if you don't set fire to that skyscraper of yours, do you think I've got the strength to burn down my house?"

Would his house remain standing? Or give in?

"Not as long as I'm still alive. I never wanted to demolish my house. It's sacred, like a part of me, and I don't want to tear myself apart limb from limb."

Give in? Never. If the idea had occurred to him it was because, like a warrior, he had briefly succumbed to fatigue.

Now, alone in his house, he kept talking. He could still hear children's cries, La Vieille's cough, the rustling of Mignonne Fleury's skirt; sometimes the floor in the Nigger's room creaked beneath the weight of invisible feet; or a tiny dry note from Cowboy's guitar, Cowboy who had gone off to discover the wide world. Dorval talked incessantly so that he wouldn't have to listen to his memories.

And his thirst was as great as his memory.

* * *

One day at noon silence burst out abruptly, as though by a detonation. Dorval ran to his window. The hammer and nails, the mechanical saws in the timber, the motors of the cranes and cement-mixers, all had stopped. He breathed on a frost-covered window to make a peep-hole. The men were coming out of the skyscraper and forming a procession. STRIKE was printed on the placards waving over their heads. WE NEED MONEY TO LIVE. SWEAT = $$$$$. Dorval pushed the window with his shoulder; the ice broke and the window opened.

"*Résistance!*" he shouted. "Resist! The people are with you. The goddam capitalists are drinking your sweat and sucking your blood. *Résistance!*"

One of the strikers came over and stared in the window.

"We want money, not a dribbling bunch of lies."

This verbal punch in the face left Dorval dumbfounded. He watched the striker put his hand into the pocket of his overalls and throw something at him but paralysed with humiliation, he couldn't avoid the egg that splattered over his face. The worker re-joined the line of protesting strikers dragging their feet through the snow. MORE MONEY = MORE MILK = HEALTHY KIDS. Dorval spat out the names of all the sacred objects he knew; then he calmed down and wiped his face.

He drank a beer.

It was a painful affront.

He drank another beer.

All his life he had been waging war against the capitalists; the affront was very painful.

He drank another beer.

Did he have the right to turn his back on this united group of exploited men?

He drank another beer.

He belonged with the workers. He went out to take his place in their procession, bored but resolved.

"*Ré-sis-tance! Ré-sis-tance!*" he chanted.

People were whispering respectfully around him.

"He's a union leader!"

"*Ré-sis-tance!*"

Soon there were dozens, a hundred mouths repeating beneath the City sky:

"*Ré-sis-tance!*"

Dorval was picked up and hoisted onto the workers' shoulders. He spread his arms and spoke to the whole world.

"The goddam capitalists are trying to throw my house to the ground; look: it's still standing. Standing there right next to their goddam skyscraper that's made out of capitalist shit and workers' blood. My dear comrades, my house is the symbol of the workers' strength that will remain standing because we're united. *Résistance!*"

The placards danced and the strikers' feet danced in the snow too, to the rhythm of the unleashed slogans.

"*Résistance! Résistance!*"

It seemed to Dorval that there was only one chest, one enormous breathing, one heart. He was exultant.

"Dorval! Dorval!"

It was a voice he knew.

"Mignonne Fleury!"

He jumped down from his triumphal perch, broke through the line, jostled the picketers and ran towards his house.

"Mignonne Fleury, have you come back?"

He wanted to put his lips on the door-step where she had placed her feet.

"Mignonne Fleury, where are you?"

Not finding her on the main floor he climbed the stairs to her room. The door was closed. He pushed it a little, politely.

"I'm bare naked. Wait a minute, you sex-fiend."

The wings of his heart were beating in their cage of bone.

"Have you come back?"

"Wait."

The door opened. Dorval opened his eyes so that he wouldn't be dazzled. He opened them again, cautiously.

"I've forgotten all about the past," she said.

No words came to Dorval's mouth. He could only repeat:

"Mignonne."

He opened his arms, but Mignonne did not rush into them.

"It's the strike," she said. "Those men are going to be walking around the skyscraper for days and nights and weeks and months."

"It's going to be a long strike. The goddam capitalists can wait. When the strikers are dying of hunger their tongues will be that long and they'll jump with joy as far as the two-thousandth floor to get hold of an ass to kiss."

"Yes, the poor people are going to be real hungry."

When she thought of them Mignonne Fleury looked distressed. Never in his life had Dorval seen such human commiseration. He was ecstatic. Mignonne Fleury wasn't a fallen woman who sold erotic tumbles and caresses and wriggles and scratches; she was being revealed to him as a victim, one who had been violated, exploited, humiliated and tortured by a voracious society. In her beautiful body, like a wild and spirited doe, a small tenacious flame was trembling: love.

"What do you think those starving men are thinking about out there while they walk around in circles like the hands of a watch?" she asked.

"A starving man cries, Vengeance; he cries, Death to Capitalists; he cries, *Nous vaincrons!*"

"Sure he says all that, but do you know what he thinks about basically?"

"About the Revolution?"

"He thinks, I want a piece of ass. And you and I, Dorval, are going to give it to him."

If a steam-hammer had fallen on his head Dorval would have been no less crushed.

"You goddam whore, you come in contact with more men than the whole length of Sainte-Catherine Street, East and West," he thought.

But when he wanted to spit those words in her face, his voice, instead of having the keen edge of insult, became all soft and said something quite different.

"The other night when I came to your room, why did you run away?"

Mignonne Fleury came to him, took his hands.

"One day, maybe."

"Do you want my house to become a bordello?"

"Would you like it better if I was against the union?"

Dorval paced back and forth between the bed and the bureau, not letting one word of his thoughts escape. Then, abruptly, the dam broke.

"There won't be no bordello in my house."

"Can't you see how sad the strikers are?"

"The whole City can get into your bed, but me, I have to sit in my chair."

"No," said Mignonne.

* * *

Someone knocked at the door. A truck-driver had just delivered a number of mattresses. Mignonne Fleury supervised their distribution in each of the rooms.

Dorval's house came back to life: the framework shuddered as though it were bursting into bloom. The roaring of the cranes and cement-mixers became like amorous sighs for Dorval; the blows of the steam-hammers and pile-drivers became sighing caresses and the mud on everyone's face became the perfume of young girls. The daily burden on the workers' shoulders was being somewhat lightened.

"Yow!" a terrified voice shouted. "A Nigger!"

Was one of the girls having her throat slit? Dorval ran to the defense of the screaming woman. Little Rosita with her pink satin bows had the pallor of death.

"A Nigger! she stammered. "A Nigger!"

Mignonne was stroking his hair like a mother. Little Rosita was hiccuping with terror.

"Everybody says Niggers are as long as that."

Rosita, in tears, held out her arms.

"Don't yell about nothing," said Dorval. "That's just one of the stories the goddam capitalists tell their daughters. The goddam capitalists want a monopoly on everything, even cunts."

"Shut up, Dorval!" Mignonne Fleury commanded. "We're in the civil service: no politics."

She stroked Rosita's cheek.

"My dear child, maybe he isn't a Nigger. Sometimes our customers are pretty dirty."

Dorval came into the room. His tenant, the Nigger, had come back. When he saw Dorval he looked down. Dorval went out and closed the door.

"We'll have to give the little girl another room."

"There's already a girl in all the rooms."

"One of the rooms will have two girls. It'll be reserved

for the union chiefs and the bosses."

The strikers with their placards, instead of looking down at the ground like tired or troubled men, now marched with their heads held high, their eyes rivetted to the windows of Dorval's house where unreal shadows sometimes appeared.

"Nous vaincrons!" they chanted. *"Nous vaincrons!"*

They never looked towards the skyscraper. MONEY FOR ALL. WE WANT JUSTICE FROM THE GROUND UP. WE WANT BREAD.

Madame Mignonne Fleury greeted her customers. She gave each one a number that corresponded to the room he had selected. Monsieur Dorval, at the cash-register, checked the numbers, established the rates and invited the customers not to stay longer than the time that had been agreed upon. Shuddering, placard in hand, they rushed to the door behind which paradise awaited them.

Sometimes when they left the customers threw away their placards.

"The union'll never give me what I just got!"

If one of the girls was free she would open her window and yell,

"Help!"

And the strikers came running.

The house was closed for a few minutes every morning. Madame Fleury and Monsieur Dorval stuck a sign on the door: "Closed for business." With a serious expression, they walked towards the City. It was always at the time when the banks opened. They came back, eager to open again.

Sometimes Dorval, at the cash-register, permitted himself to talk about politics.

"Guys, capitalism's stronger than the Union. But what you don't know is that it's capitalism that finances the unions. Do you really want to bite the tit that's feeding you?"

"Monsieur Dorval, no politics."

Madame Fleury begged him to keep his ideas to himself.

"Monsieur Dorval, you know that we are at the service of all the political parties."

He smiled his agreement and went to the refrigerator to get himself a beer, trying to stroke Mignonne Fleury's thigh as he passed her. Mignonne dodged his caress every time.

"One day . . . one day," she sighed.

Dorval's heart was pounding.

"I'm dying."

"Monsieur Dorval, the customer in no. 10 is late."

Completely docile, Dorval went and knocked at the door of no. 10, intending to claim the fee from the tardy customer. He came down again, confessing.

"Me, I've got a fire burning where you think. If that isn't love . . ."

"One day I'll give you everything you want. Everything."

Dorval took another beer and went to sit by the cash-register to check the addition on the computer-tape.

"If my house was as high as that skyscraper next door, she'd be full of customers."

"You gotta give the people what they want."

"But the goddam capitalists are the only ones that can afford to buy skyscrapers. The poor guys like us that don't make very much, the ones that weren't born with no spoon at all in our mouths, we're condemned to little businesses too."

"No politics and keep smiling, that's the motto of this house," Mignonne reminded him.

One morning Dorval was awakened in his chair by cold little fingers touching his face. He opened his eyes; it was La Vieille leaning over him, wearing a pink dress with big green flowers on it. The décolletage opened to reveal the dry fruits of her bosom.

111

"You come back to us."

"You don't know spring's here, Dorval honey? I got the hell out of the Hospice de la Sainte-Enfance. They can shut me up again when they nail me in my coffin, not before."

Dorval cleared his throat to give himself time to realize that he wasn't dreaming.

"This isn't any place for you. Times've changed. Don't think time stands still. You get old, time passes. Life goes on, changes."

"Dorval, do you know what it's like to lie in a bed that's as cold as your grave?"

"You're old. At your age you should be praying to the good Lord in case there is one on the Other Side."

Mignonne Fleury flounced out with the smiling determination of the employee who is given the task of freeing the sun for a fine day on earth.

"La Vieille wants a bed," Dorval explained.

"You should be thinking of your grave, instead of having depraved ideas like that. But you're lucky; the Shrimp can't come in today. You can take no. 9."

"When I'm in Heaven, nailed inside my coffin, I'll pray for you, my child."

Around eleven o'clock in the morning a customer asked to be taken to room no. 9. It had been enthusiastically recommended to him. Twenty minutes later another customer slipped Dorval a tip, asking for no. 9. Around noon, a few customers asked for no. 7 or no. 6, asking for Rosita, Gérardine or Philomène, but a long line of strikers was waiting their turn to go to no. 9. Realizing La Vieille's astonishing success, Mignonne Fleury decided to dismiss the Shrimp. She telephoned her.

"Hello Shrimp, sweetie. You can screw off now. I don't want to see your pretty little face in here again, okay?"

At four o'clock in the afternoon a customer asked to go to the phantom's room.

"The phantom?" asked Dorval.

"Yeah, apparently it's no. 9."

The men who were waiting in line were talking about it.

"Apparently in no. 9 you do it without even seeing the girl."

"You don't see her at all. She stays under the sheet; looks just like a ghost."

"But you can see through the sheet and tell it isn't a woman; it's the devil squeezing your prick."

These comments were repeated by one striker after another, right to the end of the line, to the very last row of picketers who were offhandedly waving their placards.

GODDAM CAPITALISTS. WE WANT MORE $$$$$.

Dorval was lightly strumming the buttons of his cash-register. At the sight of his customers' ravished faces he congratulated himself for winning his great victory over the capitalism that makes men's faces sad.

Suddenly a customer came falling down the stairs howling, holding his pants in his hands, his face pale and greenish, choking with fear. He was sweating, his nose was running, he was hiccuping, coughing, desperate. Through his coughs he could finally be heard to say:

"The phantom, the one under the sheet, she's as stiff as an icicle!"

Speaking had freed him from his terror and he could say:

"I didn't even get time to finish. I want a refund."

Dorval charged at him like a furious elephant, grabbed his testicles and threw him out the window. Thrown to the ground, the little man still demanded:

"I want a refund. I didn't even get to finish."

Upset because he had been capable of such violence, Dorval went out and bent over the little man who was putting his pants back on. He held out some bills to the man. He counted them.

"That's too much. I just want my refund. I'll never forget it as long as I live. I lifted up the sheet to see the devil underneath it. It was a real woman but she was all purple. And colder than a winter day."

Dorval locked his cash-register and ran up to no. 9. He lifted the sheet. The dead face was smiling. He removed the whole sheet. La Vieille's grey body looked like an old piece of driftwood, all dry and knotty.

"I pray to the good Lord that all the capitalists will be as thin as her when they die."

Mignonne helped Dorval put the flowered dress on the corpse and they came down again slowly, with all the majesty of those who are assisting fate. Mignonne went to the telephone.

"Hello Shrimp, love. I was just kidding before. A pretty bad joke, eh sweetie? I'm sorry. As long as I'm here you got a bed for as long as you want. So come back to us right away, okay Shrimp sweetie? I got a new trick to teach you. Something I learned from a sailor, a real Japanese sailor. It's not for everybody, no, just for girls that think with their heads. Like you, Shrimp dear. I'm going to teach you the Phantom's trick. My precious Shrimp, come over right away. There's a whole line of customers waiting. Yeah, a long line. Boy! just like a line of people waiting for confession!"

Dorval took the telephone away from her.

"Hello, Hospice de la Sainte-Enfance? This is Monsieur Dorval speaking. Would you have the kindness to be good enough to tell the people in charge there that La Vieille is dead? Her name? She didn't have a name. It was La Vieille. A name? She must have had one, but I never knew it. Do you think that stopped her from dying? Oh, she died like a saint, her arms stretched out in a cross, saying her prayers. In Latin! Oh my dear little Sister of the Sainte-Enfance, I pray you may have such a death. Amen!"

114

The Nigger's door opened.

He ran away, groaning as though pursued by fire; he ran through the snow weeping even harder. The customers waiting in line burst out laughing because the Nigger was naked. When they saw this strange black animal who looked like both a man and a nightmare, the picketers began to run after him, jostling him with their placards which they twirled in the air like idiotic birds: they scattered around behind him, shouting. The skyscraper looked like a ruin.

Dorval said, "I don't know his name neither."

"Maybe it was the soul of La Vieille," said Mignonne Fleury.

A customer raised his voice. "In any case, it isn't the soul of *Monsieur* Dorval. Because a capitalist that works in white slavery ain't got no soul."

The words hit Dorval like a bucket of urine in the face. Unable to master his limbs which were shaken in every direction by a violent electrical force, he gripped his cash-register, walked over to the man who had insulted him and hit him over the head. The bell rang at the shock, the drawer opened and coins fell out and bills, blown by the wind, flew out over outstretched hands, flew and drifted and rose up higher than the skyscraper while Dorval was held back by a net of muscular hands and arms.

"You great goddam capitalist; no violence," he heard.

He was the one they were talking to. His voice was still trembling with anger when he announced, "Today the house is free until sunset. I ain't got a capitalist heart."

The hands and arms opened and he was liberated. Only one hand still held him: it belonged to Mignonne Fleury.

"Your craziness is going to ruin our business."

"I'm not worried; even if you got your ass in a sling, you'd still have your ass."

He went inside and lovingly savoured a bottle of beer

while the customers moved around like new landlords, pushing doors open onto shouts of surprise or satisfied chuckles; they went in and out, exchanged impressions or judgements, argued like farmers at an agricultural fair. The sun sank slowly behind the horizon and the customers became impatient because soon their adventures wouldn't be free any more.

"They can say what they want, Monsieur Dorval is a great man!"

The next day a police car stopped at the door.

"Today you're shut!" a policeman announced, puffing out his chest and adjusting his cap, after almost tearing the door off its hinges.

Some other policemen ran towards strategic points where they placed themselves like the pillars of an unshakeable wall.

"The girls stay put," said the policeman with the expanded chest.

A second wave of policemen hurled themselves towards the rooms, removing the customers who came downstairs pulling up their pants — but silently, cringing in the silence.

Then another car pulled up in a cloud of dust, a long black car this time; a short man, silently bent, got out of it, wearing a bowler hat and hiding behind dark glasses. Escorted by two policemen who stopped behind him at the door, blocking it, the man ran inside. He raised his hat to Dorval.

"*Monsieur le Maire!* Welcome!" he said, bending his knees.

"This is a very great honour, *Monsieur le Maire*," said Mignonne Fleury. "Please be assured that we voted for you and that we will always vote for you."

Monsieur le Maire undid his necktie and threw it over Dorval's arm, pulled off his jacket, held out his foot to Mignonne Fleury so that she could untie his shoe-laces, stepped out of his shoes, took off his pants and threw them at Dorval, removed his shirt and finally when he was wearing nothing but his round little belly, which hung down like a loin-cloth, he demanded with authority: "No. 9 is the one I want."

"I'll take you there, *Monsieur le Maire,*" said Mignonne Fleury elegantly—that is to say, she rolled her r's elaborately.

He went upstairs singing "La donna è mobile" but he came down again furious.

"You tricked me! This is robbery! This is exploitation! No. 9 doesn't know any more than the little secretary that was in my office this morning."

"Forgive us, *Monsieur le Maire*; she's new. The other no. 9 left."

"She, she returned to her home ground," Dorval babbled.

His skull red and convulsed beneath his bowler-hat, the Mayor got dressed again and ran to his car. He picked up the telephone.

"Why is that old pile of bricks beside the skyscraper still standing? It's a blot of the landscape. And I want to protect My City. How can there be dignity without beauty?"

The policemen followed *Monsieur le Maire* like little kittens following their mother.

The strikers had stopped marching around the sky-scraper; now they were marching in neat rows around Dorval's house. The same placards bore the same slogans and insults they had borne for several weeks. The skyscraper had drifted out of their lives like a great ship that interests no one while the sailors are enjoying themselves in a pub.

One day a Radio-Canada truck pulled up and spilled out projectors, reflectors, suitcases, rolls of wire, cameras. Then a young girl appeared in the midst of the disorder holding a microphone. The strikers couldn't help thinking that she

117

could have fitted very well into one of the rooms of the house. Some other television employees selected strikers and in effeminate voices ordered them to "Stand there," "Lift your chin," "Give me a nice smile."

"Why are you on strike, my good workman?" the young girl at the microphone asked.

The striker who had been questioned took the cigar from his mouth. He could see nothing but the pendant hanging in the neckline of her blouse, and he thought of the girl in no. 9.

"Yeah, well, you see, it's like this, *calice, les Christ!*"

"And you, Monsieur?"

"Well, I guess I'd be inclined to agree with my buddy here because, well, *les hosties . . .*"

"Public opinion seems to be completely on your side, is it not, Monsieur?"

"Given the fact that I am in the public service, you will understand that even if I hope for justice I can't say so publicly; my name is Monsieur Dorval."

"And you brave men with white hair, will you pursue the battle to the end?"

"Me, I always finish what I start. My life's gonna be the first thing I gotta leave before I done all I want with it."

"To our viewers who have heard these testimonials that I do not hesitate to describe as probing, I do not believe that it would be a sin against objectivity to state publicly, before our viewers, that these men are noble in their misery and charming in their ignorance."

That evening, Dorval put his television set in the window. The strikers all came together to watch the programme, "The News of the Day." All the rooms were empty; the girls came out to join the strikers, who didn't let them have the best places.

They saw a picture of the skyscraper.

"There we are!"

The strikers swallowed their saliva and elbowed their way closer to the set. The men who had talked into the girl's microphone were trembling: their images were going to be detached from their bodies and flattened onto the screen. The skyscraper grew as though it had been blown up. A man's head filled the screen with the look of someone who is sitting on a nail but still smiles.

"For several months a gigantic skyscraper has been under construction in an area of the City formerly filled with slums. To change misery into wealth: this was the goal that was set by the Brizeco Company which holds the majority of the shares in the Companies that represent the majority of the Corporation. However . . ."

The screen went blank.

"We were too ugly, *Christ!* We blew up their Kodak."

The screen was immediately re-lit and the blonde Vicky Tomate opened her mouth:

> The season of roses
> Of lilies and flowers
> Is ours.

The makeup on her old skin was creased into a smile.

The man who was smiling on his nail returned.

"We apologize for this slight technical error. But now let us listen to Your Honour, Our Honour, His Honour the Finance Minister. The Minister has just announced a tax increase, but it is a kind of increase that is actually a reduction."

"We didn't even get to see ourselves," one of the strikers complained.

"Ah! *les Christ!*"

"We didn't hear ourselves neither."

"Ah! *les hosties!*"

119

Their anger rose in fits and starts. Dorval rushed to his set to protect it from blows.

With one movement, with one angry heart, the strikers went back to the skyscraper. They would break with clubs that goddam skyscraper made of a mixture of cement and their own sweat, their fatigue mixed with machine-oil, their disgust mingled with the grey colour of the walls.

At the front door a note from the Union announced that the strike was over. Once again, thanks to the Union, the workers had won a total victory. Hosannah! They all read the note and walked away muttering.

No one came to the house of Dorval and Mignonne Fleury. The gold-fever was over in the Klondike of the lower part of the City. One by one the girls left. Dorval was as sad as autumn when the leaves fall.

Monsieur stayed behind with Madame.

* * *

"I can't stand spring anymore," said Dorval. "Mignonne . . ."

"Dorval! You'll get me when you catch me."

Mignonne ran towards the skyscraper. The running lifted her skirt and her thighs sparkled with all their secrets. She laughed with her mouth wide open and her breasts leaped like two small warm animals.

"Catch me if you can, you big lump!"

Dorval hadn't done so much running since the war. The accumulated years were heavy in the fat of his stomach.

Mignonne made her way among the walls of the skyscraper. Dorval tried to spy her behind the piled-up cement blocks, the stacks of boards, the bags of sand piled up beneath the glaucous light from a few scattered bulbs.

"Dorval!"

He looked up. Mignonne's hair was hanging down through an opening in the ceiling.

"Come and get me!"

How had she managed to climb so high? Dorval moved forward beneath the opening. She laughed.

"I can't jump that high."

With a mocking laugh she dropped him a ladder. Dorval climbed up like a cat sniffing his prey, a very fat, out-of-breath cat. When he reached the next floor he still saw nothing but bags, boards, rolls of wire and cement blocks.

"Dorval!" Mignonne called down from the next floor, her head in the opening. Dorval walked until he was standing under her.

"Give me the ladder."

"No. If you want me that bad you should be able to jump."

All his muscles contracted. Dorval stepped back, then forward, and leaped. He felt as though the building were attached to his behind, he was so heavy.

"Give me the ladder."

"A man that needs a ladder to climb isn't a man."

She let the ladder down again. Dorval began to climb it slowly this time: if she made him climb all the way to the two-thousandth floor he'd better save his strength. He felt heavier and heavier. By the next floor he was breathing so hard he thought there was someone else there in the darkness. He didn't see Mignonne.

"Take the ladder if you want it. Me, I'm going by elevator."

He didn't have time to take a single step towards her. A catch was released and the motor started to hum. Mignonne Fleury climbed into a grille-work cage that carried her very high. Dorval listened to her laughter among the creaking of pulleys and the hissing of cables. The motor stopped. Dorval ran towards the elevator. Put his finger on the button. Waited. The motor remained silent. She hadn't sent the elevator back. He returned to his ladder and climbed to the next floor. There, he rushed to press the button. Nothing. Of course. Mignonne had blocked the elevator. He ran to the ladder to hoist himself up to the next floor where another ladder would take him to another floor. Sweat was pouring into his eyes and under his arms. He was carrying the skyscraper on his back on the foolishly fragile ladders that could break at any moment. And why were the openings in the ceilings so small? He had trouble passing through them, grazing his skin against the rough edges. All the evidence indicated that they had been made for the capitalists' skinny slaves. Dorval climbed, ran, climbed some more, sweated, swore and the ladder groaned and bent. He felt he was still on the same floor, the same ladder, the same rung, and he climbed, rushing, choking; he grew heavier and heavier; he coughed; he felt as full as a bag of sand; he was thirsty; and as he grasped the rungs he ran.

"Mignonne!"

His heart had stopped beating; it felt cold in his chest. From one rung to the next the bones in his legs got softer, his arms grew weaker. The skyscraper was rising and Dorval was staying at ground-level.

"Mignonne!"

A cold wind was blowing. There was no more ladder before him now, no more roof. He had reached the last floor. He was very high in the sky. His clothes were wet from the rain of his sweat and he was shivering with cold. There were some vertical beams that looked like dead trees.

"Catch me if you can."

Mignonne was sitting in the middle of the sky. Suffocating, with gestures that were slow as though he were at the bottom of the sea, he took a ladder, leaned it against the beam at Mignonne's feet, wedged it firmly in place and began his final assault. Mignonne took off her blouse and let it fall onto Dorval's face. He breathed her perfume for a moment and then the blouse, with its female odour, flew away. He reached another rung of the ladder. She unfastened her skirt and let it fall. He was panting.

"My handsome Dorval, you'll be dead before you get here!"

He held on, climbed, coughed, raised himself up on a horizontal beam, tottered and down below him the earth moved like the sea. Above him was Mignonne Fleury, naked as Eve, beautiful with stars all around her.

"I'm waiting for you, Dorval."

He dropped his shoes, unbuckled his belt; his pants fell down to his feet and he took off his shirt. Naked on the beam like Adam in his Eden, beneath the too beautiful eye of the night, he rushed towards Mignonne.

"I've got you, Mignonne!"

The name smelled like a pool of fresh water.

Mignonne was no longer there. She was tumbling down the ladder, taking it away. Dorval raged, not daring to gesticulate because of his nakedness which he hid now behind his hands.

"Mignonne! Mignonne Fleury!" he bleated.

It was hard to know whether the ram was furious or amorous. But all he could stab with his little horn was the starry sky. Down below, Mignonne was teasing him, picking up her clothes.

"Dorval," she said softly, "you aren't getting me."

Shipwrecked in the night, stranded on a beam, he pleaded with Mignonne. The elevator carried her away.

He wept because he had been unable to hold this beautiful dream in his arms. He cried until his lungs seemed about to burst.

"Mignonne Fleury, you're beautiful and I love you!"

He screamed loud enough to rent the sky above the City; he shouted his love; he bellowed and the words broke in his mouth. The skyscraper echoed with his pain.

"Mignonne Fleury, you're torturing me!"

Before going into Dorval's house she stopped to listen to the sad voice that was coming from the sky.

"Mignonne, I need you!"

She shuddered. She didn't dare to wipe the tear from her cheek.

There was only one way that he could free himself: Dorval let himself slide down one of the vertical beams. The descent left him with bleeding cuts on his legs and hands and stomach. He got dressed again. The elevator refused to work. Mignonne had blocked the door on the ground floor. He came down by ladder, from floor to floor. The descent seemed to take a month. It seemed as long as his Atlantic crossing.

"Jeanne! Jeanne-la-Pucelle! Wait for me!"

Getting down was as hard as climbing up. The skyscraper was swaying. Beneath his weight the ladders stretched like rubber. Dorval was weeping. What would prevent him from falling? He was tremendously tired. Dying would have seemed like sleep. Sleep—he slept and his limbs continued to descend the ladders. Just to let himself drop . . .

Suddenly there was no more ladder. He was on the ground floor. He could leave the skyscraper. Walk to his house. Resist his fatigue. The churned-up earth was breathing like a sleeping person. Dorval dropped onto his bed.

"Dorval," a voice whispered, "you've got me."

Dorval's hand touched something, a forehead, some hair or a hand.

124

"Dorval, here I am, my Dorval."

He slept and his breathing was as vast as the breathing of the whole earth beneath the night.

* * *

The strike was over so the cranes and cement-mixers tried to come back to life. The oil was cold, the steel had frozen. The gears were welded to one another in their rusted immobility. The young spring had not yet touched these machines. The workers went back to their posts here and there, shivering in the grey concrete tower where the wind was whistling. They tried to find the gestures that had become automatic to them by cursing this thing that they detested but had to build. Hunched over their machines, the mechanics were cleaning, tightening screws, soldering and blaspheming as they worked on the motors of the trucks or the bulldozers.

These cold failures with mechanical hearts that were beginning to beat again did not reach Dorval, but the shell of silence in which he was sailing was broken by the sound of knocking at his door. Were there three men before him? Two? Or only one? Someone handed him a sheet of paper. He wanted to read but the letters twisted and turned like alphabet-soup. The words *Demolition Notice*, the letters of which had stopped dancing, became very clear. It was then that Dorval saw there was only one man.

"Wait, I'm gonna go and get my, uh, wife. She's the boss here, get it?"

He took a few steps and turned around, grinning.

"She's the big gun here!"

Dorval came back carrying his rifle.

"At the count of three I let go and shoot you in the rear. One. Two. Three."

The functionary was already far away. Sheltered, he wrote out his report in seventeen copies: "Dorval House: definite architectural interest. Transfer file to Historical Monuments."

Dorval's mail-box wasn't empty that morning. He took out a yellow, blue and green postcard with trees whose foliage unfurled like a woman's hair, all down the length of a blue stream, blue as the eyes of that goddam Mignonne Fleury. "Dearest landlord, we're in Californie. Business trip. Big business. $$$. Its a sort of honeymoon too. Happiness is nice. One fight a week = $$$. We get ourselves beat up pretty bad but we make $$$. We're living in silk. Lots love. Killer and Strangler Laterreur."

"We're living in silk," Dorval repeated, laughing. "Two big whales in little silk panties."

He put down his rifle and supported his stomach with his hands because it hurt him to laugh this morning.

"Mignonne! Mignonne!"

She didn't reply. She was probably still asleep. He went up to her room and found it empty. So were her bureau drawers and her closet.

"Mignonne!"

He ran to the next floor.

"Mignonne!"

The silence in his house was so great it stifled even the rumour that came from the skyscraper.

* * *

The skyscraper stopped growing. The last sections of the walls had been lifted and put into place by the cranes. The last windows were screwed into their openings. The wind had stopped blowing. The skyscraper was closed upon itself. Electricians, plasterers, painters, decorators and

126

carpenters had begun to stir within the cocoon.

Rifle on his knees, Dorval rocked and drank his beer. Resist? How long could he go on? His old, rotten house might come falling down on him before they came to demolish it.

"Goddam pile of bricks! To hell with it. If it gets smashed it can smash me with it."

He often got up, rifle in hand, and wandered through his house, into the Laterreurs' room; he would go into the Nigger's room or, on the first floor, he would glance into the room where La Vieille used to live, push open Dupont-la-France's door and hesitate for a while in Mignonne Fleury's room. Then he would go up to the Marchessault's apartment. When he came downstairs again he wept.

"Can a man go on resisting when he's all alone, alone like Christ on the cross?"

His house was filled with the grey shadow of silence. He had thrown a bottle at the television set. Even the rotten wood of the framework had stopped crackling.

"Landlord baby we're in the Mexican sun. $$$. It's like a long honeymoon. We both got a black eye. The sun brings out everything that's good in men. Love Killer and Strangler Laterreur."

He wept.

He would resist.

"That skyscraper's going to come down because it was goddam capitalists that built it. A capitalist that sells sand mixes gray dirt in with it. A capitalist that sells cement puts sand in his cement. A capitalist that sells steel mixes scrap-iron in with the alloy. But in the end the thing stands. How come? Because we got a capitalist system. Anywhere else in the world, *Mesdames et Messieurs,* under another kind of régime, that skyscraper would splatter like a cow-pie."

Dorval was alone.

127

During the war he had been alone too.

The war was all around him, but the grass was as peaceful as the blue silence of the sky. He was alone in an immense tranquillity where he could have drowned himself; a shot could go off under him, he often thought, as he lay there on the cool earth: one shot and the earth would open beneath him and he would be drowned. He was alone and at the thought he began to breathe faster; he knew though, that behind the next hill another man was stretched out on the ground listening to his breathing too, thinking that the earth could cover him with an eternal wave; and further away there was Jeanne-la-Pucelle.

"Mignonne Fleury!"

Dorval was alone but he wouldn't give in, not to the capitalists and not to solitude.

"Men are always alone in this goddam life. Look at them piled up, sticking together: kittens on their mother's belly. Look at them sucking at the crowd. They're all alone. Look at them hanging on to women that are going to give them a life that tastes of sour milk. They're more scared of living alone than wasting away with some woman. Men are alone on this earth: look at how they surround themselves with kids, the way you make a hill around a potato-plant. Ah! *Petit Jésus de Dieu!* the only time I wasn't alone was when I was fighting. And how about you, Jeanne-la-Pucelle, are you still in the Resistance? I know the war's over but we haven't got the world Revolution yet, Jeanne. Jeanne, are you on the same side as me?"

During the days he watched over his territory, rifle in hand. The skyscraper's shadow was as heavy as death to come.

"Dorval! Dor - or - val!"

He looked up. Hundreds of windows all in straight lines reflected the setting sun; the skyscraper was a dazzling gigantic mirror.

"It's me, Mignonne!"

The voice came from the sky that was reflected by the walls of the skyscraper.

"Mignonne Fleury!"

"Yes. I'm in 2551."

"2551?"

"Yes."

"On the two-thousandth floor?"

"Yes."

Dorval threw down his rifle and ran towards the skyscraper where a porter wearing a red uniform and white gloves opened the door for his with an obsequiousness that Dorval took for contempt.

"The two-thousandth floor?"

"Monsieur means . . ."

"2551. Where's the ladder?"

"If Monsieur will kindly follow me."

The porter opened the elevator door for him.

* * *

Dorval moved forward in a musical penumbra that was diffused by concealed lamps. He wished he could slow down the beating of his heart. He was panting too, as much as he had when he climbed this height floor by floor, rung by rung. His skin, shivering, felt prickly under his sweat.

"Come here!"

Mignonne Fleury was adrift in a lacy foam in a bed that looked like a throne. There were bits of lace quivering at the windows too, that were open to the night. The walls were pink, soft pink, flesh pink and the light caressed the shadows that fell on them.

"Mignonne Fleury!" Dorval sighed, paralysed, on the verge of tears, his outstretched hands trembling.

"Are your boots clean?" Mignonne worried.

Her poisonous words bit his foot that was placed on the white carpet. He stepped back. His hands stopped trembling. He breathed more calmly.

"Mignonne!"

"Go take a shower. I don't want your dirty feet in my skyblue sheets."

In despair, he turned his back. Should he jump out the window and disappear into the void? He decided to take the elevator.

"Goddam capitalist!"

His house was waiting faithfully for him beneath the weight of its years. With its broken window-panes it looked abandoned. The roof was bent under its rot. All the beams could have been torsoes in the old skeleton.

He raised both fists towards the skyscraper.

"Goddam capitalists, before that pile of bricks of yours is as rotten as mine there'll be lots more capitalists to demolish you."

The skyscraper remained mute but somewhere someone was picking notes off a guitar. He listened. Cowboy? Dorval ran. Had Cowboy come back?

> I crossed over rivers
> Carrying my songs
> But nobody liked them
> So I tried the towns
> But even in town
> They didn't like my songs.

Dorval shouted, "Cowboy! Welcome to my place! Come and get drunk with me! Cowboy!"

A few sad notes replied.

> The trees and the roads and the sky
> All told me: don't sing

"Cowboy! Come and celebrate your return to the fold. You're the first one, Cowboy!"

Dorval picked up his mail and put a bunch of beer bottles on the table. Cowboy was silent. His fingers were seeking a melody on the strings of his guitar and his voice was looking for a song.

> The trees and the road and the sky
> They all told me: don't sing
> But I wanna sing, so I can feel alive.

Dorval drank a bottle. He looked at the sea, the beach and the palace on the edge of the mountain that was clothed in palm-trees and roses; he turned over the postcard that the Laterreur Brothers had sent from Brazil.

"Brazil! *Baptême du Christ!* And I'm stuck here in my goddam coffin."

He read: "The sun fills our hearts and the Brazilian samba makes our bodies shrudder and the moneys pouring into our pockets like fallen leafs in Canada. We made our little love-nest in a pink Cadillac but Strangler didn't like the colour and we painted the top yellow and the hubcaps green. We're looking for a driver if the job interests you please send application to Laterreur Inc."

"Damn goddam capitalists!"

He tore the card to shreds, threw them to the floor and stamped on them. Cowboy had turned around. He burst into a happy song.

> In the air
> On the ground
> Can't make a sound
> So we hide
> Underground.

131

Dorval drank. Rocked.

"Mignonne, why the hell didn't I wash my goddam feet? Do you know why?"

He rocked and drank for a long time. Then he fell asleep.

The rolling of his chair carried him away in the night.

Dorval was walking in a straight line among some other *Résistants.* They heard nothing but the silence of the moss and the leaves and the sky. Someone whispered the order to halt:

"A minute to rest by the river. No smoking. We'll be seen."

The men took off their shoes and soaked their feet in the cool water. A few let themselves slide into the water.

"Come with me."

The warm voice of Jeanne-la-Pucelle whispered these words into Dorval's ear. He picked up his rifle and followed her. All around her the night was gentle, it smelled like a woman's hair. He put out his hand to touch her thigh.

"I forbid you to look at me."

She undressed and got into the water. With his back turned to the river he heard the waves splashing against her body; he could hear her breathing like a woman who is in love. Dorval shivered. She came back to the river-bank.

"You're beautiful."

"I forbade you to look at me."

She came out of the water and put her clothes back on.

"It isn't prudent to swim by yourself," she explained.

"Do you think it's prudent to expose a man to dizziness like you just did? My heart's going like a boxer's fist, clenching and unclenching."

She put her hand on Dorval's chest.

"It's true," she said, "it's beating very hard."

"And yours?"

132

Dorval moved his hand to put it on La Pucelle's bosom. She smiled. "There's a war on."

Dorval walked ahead of her because he didn't want to go crazy watching Jeanne's long hair sway, her haunches dance before him, watch the night pitching like the sea.

He stopped abruptly and pointed his rifle at the sky.

"Don't shoot, idiot!"

She grabbed his hand, all furious claws. He laughed unpleasantly.

"I just felt like making a little noise."

Jeanne loosened her grip. "Don't you think there are already too many men making noises on this earth tonight?"

In the distance the immense wheel of the war was spinning. Dorval heard a shout. "I got it! I got my diploma!"

The night swung violently into day. Barnabé Marchessault was standing before Dorval.

"I got my diploma!"

Barnabé pulled a paper out of the back pocket of his trousers and unfolded it.

"My official diploma!"

Dorval tore himself out of his chair but the night was still clinging to him.

"That's nice, very nice," he said, coughing.

Barnabé was jubilant. He pulled Dorval outside.

The first thing Dorval saw in front of his door was a wall of steel: the blade of a bulldozer, with Hildegarde triumphant on top of it, her thighs gleaming in the sun, among her dozen whining children. Barnabé climbed onto the tractor and started it with expert movements and knowing gestures.

"I'm the one that's gonna demolish you."

Barnabé speeded up. The motor roared like a victorious beast.

"Inside every poor man's pants there's a capitalist asshole hiding," Dorval spat.

133

He thought of Cowboy.

"Cowboy! Our time's up. They're demolishing."

Dorval ran upstairs. Pounded on the door.

"Get out, they're demolishing!"

Cowboy had left, or he was asleep. Dorval pushed the door open. The guitar was leaning against the chair, his hat was on the floor. Cowboy was in the closet.

"*Salut*, Cowboy. You're looking pretty sad this morning."

Dorval was thunderstruck. The guitar string with which Cowboy had hanged himself had almost cut through his neck.

Dorval picked up Cowboy's hat, took his guitar and went out without speaking to the Marchessault family on their bulldozer.

He looked up at Mignonne Fleury's window. There were gardeners sticking plastic flowers into the new grass around the skyscraper. One of them looked like Dupont-la-France. Dorval smiled at the thought of Dupont-la-France fussing with plastic flowers.

What did Cowboy's last song say?

Dorval thought it might come back to him if he put Cowboy's hat on his head.